WHY THEY KILLED BIG BOY
AND OTHER STORIES

BY
MICHAEL PERRY

WHISTLERS AND JUGGLERS PRESS
P.O. BOX 1346
EAU CLAIRE, WI 54702-1346

ISBN: 0-9631695-3-X

Address all editorial correspondence
and orders for additional copies of this book to

Whistlers and Jugglers Press
P.O. Box 1346
Eau Claire, WI 54702-1346

e-mail correspondence and inquiries:
mikperry@win.bright.net

PRINTED IN THE UNITED STATES OF AMERICA

First Printing	11/96	5C
Second Printing	7/03	MD

Book and Cover Design: Frank Smoot

Cover: Illustration by Frank Smoot, ink on acid-free paper,
inspired by "Big Boy," a trademark of Elias Brothers Restaurants

CREDITS

"Shooting the Split" originally appeared as "Shooting the Split on the Drive Home" in *The Christian Science Monitor*, August 1, 1995.

A similar version of "Big Things" first appeared as "Larger than Life" in the July, 1996 issue of *The World & I*; the version within is reprinted with permission from *The World & I* magazine, a publication of the Washington Times Corporation.

A similar version of "Houses on Hills" first appeared in *Orion*; the version within is reprinted with permision from *Orion*.

At press time, "Fighting Fire" was scheduled to appear as "Response" in *National Fire & Rescue*, and appears here with permission of that publication.

A similar version of "Fighting Fire ... In Belize" originally appeared as "Fire Fighting Services in Belize" in *911* magazine, July/August 1996.

"Steve Earle, Hard-Core Troubador" originally appeared as a concert review in *No Depression*, Summer, 1996, under the byline of Michael Ryan.

"The Moon Brings Not Pleasure" originally appeared as "May we all meet there" in *The HighGround*, issue seven, under the byline of Michael Ryan.

"Aaron Tippin: A Holler Full of Trucks" originally appeared as "Aaron Tippin: A Workin' Man's Workin' Trucks" in *Road King*, August/September 1996.

"Hirsute Pursuits" originally appeared in *The Toastmaster*, June, 1995, under the byline of Michael Ryan.

"Steve Gunderson and the Game of Politics" originally appeared in *Wisconsin West*, June, 1995, under the byline of Michael Ryan.

"Life in the Fat Lane" originally appeared in *Wisconsin West*, February, 1996, under the byline of Michael Ryan.

"A Day with Dave" originally appeared in *Wisconsin West*, October, 1995, under the byline of Michael Ryan.

"Workin' on the Road Gang" originally appeared in in *Road King*, August/September 1996.

BECAUSE SOME FOLKS HAVE ASKED . . .

When I first began writing, I frequently used the name Michael Ryan, and did so until very recently. Why? There were a couple of reasons, neither of them especially interesting. But for one significant reason, the pen name itself was meaningful to me.

When I was casting about for one, I knew I didn't want a pseudonym the likes of "Michael Diamond" or "Destiny Arisen." I wanted something unobtrusive and simple, but of meaning. In the end, I settled on Michael Ryan, in memory of my sister, Rya.

Rya came to our family when she was two weeks old. She had Down Syndrome and congenital heart and lung defects. For the next five years, through numerous surgeries and setbacks, she was, as my father put it, "a trouper." Unaware of the definitive distinction, I always imagined he meant a resolute, marching soldier; a "trooper." I can still see her, an oxygen mask for her and one for her doll, leaning against a small bench in a position that eased her breathing, watching our farm family at the end of the day, clowning as much as her lungs would allow. Rya died when she was five. The influence she had on our lives runs too deeply to describe — at least I am inadequate to the task. Let me simply say her spirit remains woven through our lives.

As I began to sneak a few things into publication here and there, I got the occasional note from an editor saying there were already some Michael Ryans out there, writers far more established than I. Lately there has been more confusion. So, I've returned to the name on my tax return, and that's fine. But for one last time in print, here's to the little trouper.

She still shows me how to march.

CONTENTS

SHOOTING THE SPLIT

The truck winds around and down the on-ramp, picking up speed gradually and with effort, a fat gray beetle trundling into place among more nimble vehicles; scurrying two-doors, purposeful sedans, predatory sports cars. The kingpins are ancient, and float in their sockets; I must constantly nudge the steering wheel — left, right, left — to keep on line. I tuck the truck in the slow lane, keeping my foot tight to the floor. The pitch of the fourth-gear whine rises, climbing in harmony with the heavy roar of the six cylinders spinning behind the squat iron grille. The lugs on an out-of-season set of snow tires thrum against the concrete, setting the streetlights to dancing in the rear-view mirror.

My truck is an ugly truck. A "'51 'Binder," the farmers call it, recalling a time when the International Harvester Company made corn binders, not homely pickups. A country boy attending college in the city, I couldn't believe my luck when I picked it up for $150 from a man hauling wood. Monumentally unwieldy, it is constructed from thick slabs of rolled iron. "Gimme ten acres and I'll turn that thing around!" a laughing farmer once told me. Originally a hearty red, the truck had been swathed at some point with a pinkish coat of primer by a man named Ron. Ron used a fat paint brush and saw fit to sign and date his runny work, daubing a Playboy bunny beneath the spare tire for good measure. The truck's exterior is copious with rust, but the pink primer dominates; hints of original red show through the thin spots. The fenders are great plowshares, turned inward, prepared to till the wind. The hood rises from between the fenders like the prow of a capsized boat, a strip of pitted chrome for a keel. I have owned this truck for over a decade; in that time I have driven it everywhere, double-clutching through the city, rattling the muffler off on the way to job interviews, shouldering accountants and clerical workers aside during the rush hour — all the while unspooling a long limbo of miles left undocumented by a broken odometer. For all those city miles, however, that truck and I were always at our best when we were rolling up Five Mile Road, northbound at 3 a.m., dropping down Nadelhoffer Hill to roar through the middle of Keysey Swamp, waking the ducks, whipping curls in the salty-sweet marsh fog. Rolling north. Rolling home. And now, on this trip, I am rolling home again; this time to stay. I settle into the torn bucket seat — transplanted from a moribund Ford Maverick — rest my palm on the shift tree, and let the flick, flick, flick of the centerline unroll the road.

The truck and I drive this road well. It is the road north. The road home. This road leads to a town where greasy-capped men with dirty fingernails sit in a cafe half the morning and shake dice for coffee; a town where the fire trucks are manned by farmers and butchers; a town where Main Street is just that. At the northern edge of this town, the road splits. Curving to the left, the highway. Straight on, Five Mile Road. The truck and I will shoot the straight shot, shoot for home. Home, my house, is not on Five Mile Road. But it is at the Five Mile Road split that I begin to recognize the air. At the split I feel the *place* more than the road. At the split, I will have made it back.

I understand the dangers of returning. At first, the cafe will fall silent when I push the door open on their coffee and dice. I will sit at a table by the wall, not at the counter. The waitress will ask how I want my eggs. But in time, after I help put out a winter's worth of chimney fires, after I serve potato salad at the smelt feed, after folks get used to seeing my truck parked at the old Gravunder place, my eggs will show up over easy, no questions. But it all begins with shooting the split.

The Five Mile Road split has always been my point of re-entry; I always feel as though I am dropping down through the thin air of unfamiliar places to settle firmly in my native atmosphere. In a "hold, please" age of obfuscation and hindrance, of suffocating regulation and oversight, of congested highways and infarcted byways, there is nothing so satisfying as rocketing directly to the heart of a thing, and I have never backed off the accelerator at the split; if anything, I feed the horses, let'em run. In one beautiful kinetic moment, the truck leaves the banked curve of the highway, dips down and to the right, and I am locked in a split-second free-fall; then the wheels bounce back, and I am flying down Five Mile Road. No forms to fill out. No credit check. No "press the pound sign to repeat the menu." I simply hold to the right, shoot the split, and I am home.

Back on the interstate, darkness has fallen. The truck's six-volt headlights are weak and shaky, not so much shining as leaking on the concrete. Delineators sweep past, a perpetual regiment of one-eyed sentinels. Every mile a flourescent green marker hoves in view and flicks from sight. The heat from the engine rolls up through the steel, warming my boot. The hometown exit comes in view. I hold to the right and run the truck up and off the interstate. Beyond the stop sign, the town water tower stands as it ever did, the American flag quiet and well lit at its peak. I roll the truck down Main Street. The night before homecoming, we would snake dance down this street, a human cable, curling and snapping through town to the football field, where we circled a bonfire of old lumber and outhouses.

The three bars along the highway are dark. Double-clutching and shifting to third, I am already on the outskirts of town. One more gear, and the split comes into view. Except there is no split. The split is gone.

I smelled trouble a year or so ago when the new road signs went up. "Carlson Corners" became $3^{1}/_{2}$ Ave. "The Dirt Road" became 287th Ave. Even Five Mile Road got a number. The county justified the move with vague platitudes about preparation for a 911 system, but nothing came of it. Grass fire or heart attack, you still have to dial the seven-digit number for the fire hall. At least the street signs could be ignored. Nobody called Carlson Corners $3^{1}/_{2}$ Ave. But this business of the split is not so easily disregarded.

Apparently, some engineer somewhere, no doubt in collusion with an insurance actuary and an attorney or two, figured out that "V" splits create dangerous intersections, and had to go. As a result, the "V" split at Five Mile Road has been converted. The free-falling exhiliration of re-entry has been exchanged for a benign 90-degree turn entered at the apex of the curve. With a turn lane, of all things. There will be no more shooting the split. I downshift.

I angle into the turn lane slowly, regretfully, shaking my head. The truck growls through the right angle turn, sullen in second gear. Nadelhoffer Hill waits and here we are at ten miles an hour. I flatten the foot feed, giving the truck all it can eat; it shudders and roars, gathers itself. I nudge the wheel — left, right, left — and hold it square on the centerline. We're picking up speed. Me and this truck, we're gonna roll the fog off the Keysey. Make those ducks think we never even slowed down.

BIG THINGS[1]

The literature of the crude, instinctual colossus appealed to an urban audience by virtue of exoticism and, perhaps, fanciful nostalgia, the implicit contrast between the American Adam and the cosseted society that craved word of his untrammeled exploits. The giant was always a significant other, from another kind of place.

- Karal Ann Marling, in *The Colossus of Roads*

Thank you for your inquiry requesting information about our "Fiberglass People Attractors." Enclosed please find our price list and brochure showing some of the hundreds of items that we make. As you can see, we can make anything Large or Small.

- Jerome A. Vettrus, president of F.A.S.T. Corp.
(from a letter accompanying sales brochures)

I do want the F.A.S.T. Corp. to know that we are very proud of the New Giant Skier Statue. We have already received a tremendous amount of publicity from the skier and know it will be a huge promotional asset now and always. Again we thank you for your fine and detailed work.

- satisfied customer, in letter to Jerome Vettrus

Big Boy stood six feet tall. Weighed 300 pounds. Stood there grinning at Toledo with that double burger hoisted high, those big blue eyes round as bowling balls, those red-checkered overalls fit to bust, that flip pompadour big enough to surf. When the men — boys, really,

---

[1]Although the version of this piece which appeared in *The World & I* was entitled "Larger Than Life," I submitted it as "Big Things." Upon reflection, I believe I may have stolen this title from an album of the same name by Molly & the Heymakers. The album-cover art features Spooner, Wisconsin's legendary "Mel," a giant cowboy who, if memory serves, formerly stood tall at a Texaco. If you like funky fiddles, big guitars, and your dairy products laced with twang, check out the music my friends and fellow cheeseheads Molly and Andy make in their milkhouse by dropping a line to Muskie Queen Music, P.O. Box 1160, Hayward, WI 54843.

ten of them — showed up in the darkness, Big Boy's expression never changed. They ripped his feet from the concrete; he kept grinning. They tossed him in the back end of a pickup; he kept grinning. When the truck pulled up to an apartment on the west side of Toledo, he was still grinning.

Then things got ugly.

"What're we gonna do with him?" said one of the men. A number of suggestions were made. None caught anyone's perverse fancy. After all, pulling stunts with the Toledo Big Boy wasn't somebody's big new idea. "Nine times out of ten, if the Big Boy is missing, he's usually down at the University of Toledo," restaurant manager David Nelson would say upon discovering his missing mascot. "During fraternity season, they do that as a prank." The ten men huddled again. Then one spoke.

"Chop him up!"

And chop him up they did. A hacksaw was secured. Fiberglass particles filled the air. Big Boy's head tumbled from his neck. Then an arm came loose, severed at the shoulder. Next, a leg. When the bone-hollow sawing sounds ceased, only Big Boy's hamburger remained intact.

In a macabre twist, the first to learn of Big Boy's death by dismemberment (after the bandits) were members of his own family. At Big Boy restaurants throughout Toledo, his brothers looked down in the pale first light of morning to see bits of their luckless relative at their feet. A head, an arm, a leg, each tagged with the message, "Big Boy is Dead." At one restaurant, Big Boy's severed right buttock was discovered with a newspaper ad taped in place: "Strip Steak $2.29 a pound." Not a good way to start the day, espying bits of a family member in the

yard. Nonetheless, the relatives have maintained their sunny disposi-
tions. Grinning like Big Boys, all of'em.

As often happens in cases where criminals show off, criminals feel
the need to talk, and two weeks after Big Boy bit it, his killers were
corralled. Big Boy was worth about $4,000, and it is safe to say that will
be divided ten ways. It seems unlikely that anyone will do any hard
time, although one of the suspects, a Mr. Martinez, may wish to do so
and apply it toward his degree; he is a criminal-justice major at the
University of Toledo.

The point of this parable, however, is not the fate of the perps. Nor
do I wish to further flog the fanciful notion of oversized fiberglass figure as decedent. The significance of Big Boy as part of colossal Ameri-
cana kitsch, however, is worth pondering. Why did the abduction and
subsequent mutilation of a mass-produced corporate logo attract national press attention in publications ranging from *People* to *The New
Republic*? Why do we care about big things that really aren't big things
at all? Would we have cared if someone abducted a set of Golden
Arches? Hacked up an Arby's sign? Not likely. But take an object we
are all familiar with, blow it out of scale, and suddenly we are fasci-
nated by it. Or at least most of us are, the odd criminal justice major
excepted. But why? In *The Colossus of Roads*, Karal Ann Marling offers
the following considerations:

> Regardless of its particular purpose, the colossus is always a place
> in itself — a stopping place in time, where the everyday rules of
> reality are suspended and an idyllic dream commences. Gro-
> tesque scale demands a pause — for edification, for commerce,
> or for the fantastic fun of it.

The pause. That's it. That's why they stick giant Big Boys on top of restaurants. That's why the Freshwater Fishing Hall of Fame in Hayward, Wisconsin, is housed in a 145-foot-long, walk-through fiberglass muskellunge. So you'll pause. And when the good citizens of Rothsay, Minnesota, got together in 1976 and built themselves a 9,000-pound replica of a male prairie chicken posed in the throes of a mating dance, they for dang sure figured on getting people to pause. To quote Marling again:

> The publicity value of roadside curiosities, it would seem, increases in direct proportion to their curiousness.

Homemade 9,000-pound prairie chickens in love — now that's curiousness. But what qualifies as collosi? Marling sniffs at the idea of Big Boy as colossus. "He's actually quite small...six feet tall, I believe." Yes. But he weighs 300 pounds and perches atop restaurants. As boys go, that's colossal.

Some colossi are unmistakably colossal. Like the 15-foot-tall Paul Bunyan built on the shore of Lake Bemidji, in Minnesota. The winter of 1937 had been hard on the citizens of Bemidji; the mercury plunged to record depths and took business with it. Alternately fretting and telling tall tales around backroom stoves, the locals hit upon an idea. Why not enlist the services of a tall tale hero of the times, Paul Bunyan, to lure commerce back to the frozen Bemidji environs? And so the hardy Bemidjians whacked together an ungainly, oversized Bunyan. It worked. Paul (joined one year later by a giant mobile Babe the Blue Ox mounted on a Model A chassis) got people to stop. To pause.

In 1978, the citizens of Blue Earth, Minnesota, paused — together with the governor, Miss Minnesota, and Miss America — to watch as a

50-foot Jolly Green Giant rose high over their little town. The Jolly Green Giant took his place on a hut-sized concrete pedestal right at the location and time the eastern and western ends of I-90, the longest freeway in America, were joined. The cars flying by on the clean white concrete had little reason to stop in Blue Earth. Local merchants hoped the Giant would make the difference.

One of the largest and most uniquely functional colossi in America is the aforementioned Hall of Fame muskie in Hayward. Half a city block long and five stories tall, the "Giant Walk-Thru Muskie" dominates the Hall of Fame grounds. Visitors can ascend from within the fish to stand in its gaping maw, far above the ground. A number of couples have wended their way through the bowels of this gargantuan fish to be wedded in the lower lip. Looking into each other's eyes, the bride and groom pledge themselves to a lifetime of loving and cherishing while neatly framed by a predatory hedge of knee-high teeth.

If the Jolly Green Giant ate hamburgers, he'd probably want the one sitting in the grass along Highway 21, just east of Sparta, Wisconsin. Trimmed with cheese and fat dollops of ketchup, the burger is roughly the size of a Volkswagen. A few feet away, an ice cream cone large enough to hold Rush Limbaugh (sans ego) collects rainwater. The cone is shadowed by an elephant, and two porpoises to the north, Atlas rises against the sky, crouched as though he had the weight of the world on his shoulders, despite the fact that the world lies in fiberglass pieces at his sandaled feet. Behind Atlas and his shattered world, a great unpainted menagerie ranges around a two-acre grassy clearing: reclining bears, laughing dolphins, a seal big as a steer, a steer big as a corn crib. A six-foot Michelob bottle is canopied by chokecherries. A

25-foot tall "beach boy" lies flat on his back, with one hand extended to the sky. The hand is cupped in the form of a "C," ready to cradle a giant can of beer.

Throughout the clearing, stacked and leaned amongst the figures, are strange husk-like sections of fiberglass. From the outside, they suggest the shape of familiar things, but the lines are obscure and rough. Closer inspection reveals that the underside of each husk is finely detailed; these are the forms used to create six-foot six-packs, elephantine elephants, giant fish, giant giants — whatever your heart desires, in gargantua. Dropped at the feet of the creatures they created, the brownish forms take on the appearance of freshly-shed exoskeletons.

Stepping through the exoskeletons, reconciling the adjacent Wisconsin corn fields with the presence of a supine, grinning whale, the curious visitor might likely overlook the narrow, unassuming concrete block shed at the edge of the field. Two large red fiberglass letters stand out against the white-painted blocks: "F.A." Missing are an "S" and "T"; together the four letters stand for "Fiberglass Animals, Statues & Trademarks." There have been three fiberglass companies in Sparta since the late '50s. The first, Stouffer's Advertising, originated as a sign company. When a California company hit upon the idea of promoting their restaurants with a sculpted caricature of an "all-American boy," Stouffer's got the job. Thus was Big Boy born, and thus did Sparta begin its run as the nation's primary source of fiberglass sculpture.

When Lady Bird Johnson crusaded to rid the nation's highway of all things unsightly during the late '60s, times got tough for billboard companies. Armed with their experience creating Big Boys, Stouffer's converted to the production of "dimensional animals and statues" exclusively. In 1975, the company changed hands and operated until 1983 as Creative Display. It was during this time that the Jolly Green Giant and giant muskie were created. In 1983, Creative Display artist Jerry Vettrus became president and owner of the firm, which then became known as F.A.S.T. Corp.

"I got into it by accident," says Vettrus. His office is a narrow, cramped affair, stacked high with paperwork, scattered with statuettes of past and present projects. The walls are papered with pictures of his creations. And he did get into his profession by accident. It all began when he drew a picture of a dead dog.

"I had no formal training," he says. He is low-key and unassuming, but speaks with one eye on the clock, in the manner of a man who has much to do. "A friend's dog died, and he asked that I draw him a picture of it. I did. And then I was an artist.

"Eventually, I had some of my work for sale in a cafe, and the owners of Creative Display saw it. They asked me to do some artwork for them. Then in 1976 they asked me to run the plant."

Today, Vettrus has fourteen employees, and business is brisk — a fact over which he is mildly despairing. "I am a combination business-man/artist by necessity," he says ruefully, riffling a stack of government forms on his desk. "Of course I'd rather just be an artist."

The bulk of F.A.S.T. Corp. business comes from water parks, which order trailerfuls of hippo drinking fountains, gorilla swings, crawl-thru fish, whale fountains, and turtle slides. The company also supplies figures for miniature golf courses, civic projects, playgrounds, lawn decoration, and national brand promotions.

Despite the fact that F.A.S.T. has a collection of over 500 molds, Vettrus receives roughly one dozen requests for new items each year. "You just tell me what size you want of it," he grins. When a new project is commissioned, the object is photographed from the front and side, then "blown up" using a system of grids. Next, the front and side profile cutouts are constructed in full-size from 5x12 sheets of cardboard taped together. The cutouts are then joined at bisecting right angles and sprayed with carvable foam. The foam is sculpted (faces and hands are sometimes sculpted from clay for greater detail), plastered, spray-painted, and then coated with wax. A fiberglass casting is then made. When it hardens, it is cut away. The original model is destroyed in the process.

A similar process is then used to make the actual statue. The cast form is sprayed with wax, then fiberglass. After removal from the form, the statue is trimmed and sanded, then painted. "We use automotive paint," says Vettrus, "so once they're done, we just bolt'em down to the trailer and roll down the highway."

"I do more of the detail sculpting — hands and faces — and the painting," says Vettrus. "If you want to know more about the initial sculpting, you should visit Oz." "Oz," as it turns out, is longtime friend and fellow sculptor Dave Osborne. "He's out in the industrial park across town carving a 25-foot gorilla."

Dave Osborne is in his fifties. He has been sculpting colossi of one form or another since 1962. "It's all I ever done," he'll tell you. Today he is standing on a stepladder, wielding an electric coping saw. Bits of foam cling to his sweatshirt, dot his hair, gather on his thick eyebrows as he carves out the waist of his 25-foot gorilla. Across the workshop the gorilla's unfinished torso holds its arms high and wide, as if hoisting a giant beer keg over its head. The sculpture is too tall for the building and must be constructed in two halves.

"My background, as far as the sculpting?" says Osborne, lowering his saw. "Ummm...nothing, really. I learned to work with large size and shape through the billboard business. Learned how to scale things up. Nothing formal. I didn't take no schooling of any source." He is a stocky man, self-effacing but eager to describe his work.

"The hardest part is you got to have a photographic mind." He picks up an air wrench, presenting it in side and front view. "For instance, if you pick up an object like this and say 'OK, make this ten feet tall,' that's fine, they can give you a picture of it and you can make the cutouts, but you still have to have a heck of an imagination what the missing parts look like. It's like this ape. Unless you have an ape sitting right here, you have to fill in the detail."

Then, as if he has made it all sound too difficult, he grins. "Aww, we just grid it up." He waves a dismissive hand. "It's just like building airplanes."

America, the country where we do everything bigger and better, seems a natural for colossi — and indeed, America does seem to have cornered the market on kitschy colossi, although Karal Ann Marling points out that second place in the colossus race traditionally goes to totalitarian regimes. "They don't tend to be popular. They are often designed to stun rather than impress. Saddam Hussein designed a Gulf War Memorial in the shape of giant hands holding a scimitar above the citizens of Iraq." I'll take the prancing prairie chicken, thanks.

But is there room for giant things in America anymore? Sometimes it seems most of our modern colossi are conceptual: the Internet is a perfect example. Will people still pull off the road to look at an acromegalous cow? Karal Ann Marling doesn't think so. "There are not a lot of new ones being built. We've gotten just a little more sophisticated than 'big equals interesting.'" But Vettrus and Osborne disagree.

"We don't promote a lot, but every year it seems like we do something for a city or a community," says Vettrus. "Seymour, Wisconsin, is the hamburger capital of the world, and they just called me and want to rent our giant 11-foot hamburger for three months this summer...and if they like it, they may end up buying it for the city.

"When they're traveling, people just love to stand next to something and have their picture taken. It highlights their trip and gives them a remembrance of where they've been. Something that's larger than life-size is interesting.

"It's a photographic thing."

Dave Osborne is standing beside an unfinished gorilla toe the size of a third grader. You can't convince him the hunger for colossi in America has died. "It's simple. It turns heads. It's like the Big Boy they had there for a while. He had that hamburger...it was simple."

Despite the upbeat spin of Vettrus and Osborne, hints of change are afoot. Increasingly restrictive ordinances regarding signage have caused many Big Boy restaurants to opt for simple, one-dimensional illuminated emblems. The demand for full-sized Big Boys has tailed off, and F.A.S.T. Corp. stopped making them several years ago. Back in Toledo, they've patched Big Boy the murder victim back together as best they can. His stomach and one ear are still missing, however, and out in front of the restaurant he so proudly represented, his concrete footprints remain unfilled.

HOUSES ON HILLS

*The good building makes the landscape more beautiful than it was before
that building was built.*
                                                    - Frank Lloyd Wright

It was the ship-shaped house that finally did it. In the space of a
few short months, it came plowing over the crest of a formerly mapled
hill, the beveled two-story prow of the living room looming into the
skyline like a grounded destroyer jammed atop a sand dune. During
my weekly comings and goings, I watched it take shape, and won-
dered what had moved the owner to choose this particular site. Ego,
perhaps, an ostentatious hankering to let folks know that this particular American dream was charging right along. But if conspicuous consumption explains the view he's given us, it hardly explains the one
the owner has chosen for himself: a glittering, bi-level bank of garage-
door-sized windows affording an unobstructed, panoramic view of ...
the freeway. On any given summer weekend, the owner of this nauti-
cal monstrosity can chill a drink, retire to the balcony, and review an
endless parade of Illinois tourists pell-melling their way north.

In his recent book, *Mapping the Farm* (Knopf), author John
Hildebrand refers to this new trend in home building as the "look at
me" school of architecture. By my definition, look-at-me hill houses
are largish new homes constructed on former farmland, atop hills. The
trend seems to be to hack a square out of the treeline, deposit the house,
and dam the horizon. In even more egregious instances, there are no

trees at all; the house squats solo on the skyline, subtle as a gopher mound on a putting green.

People are entitled to displays of bad taste. Heck, I'm the last person to judge someone on matters aesthetic — me, sitting here in my sweatpants in a one-armed office chair at a discount-chain desk constructed of particle board and wood-grain contact paper. But at least I'm not perched on a hill beside the interstate, big as a house. It's one thing to exhibit a complete lack of style and grace in the privacy of your own home. It's entirely another thing to do it at the expense of everyone's landscape. These people don't want to be part of the horizon, they want to *be* the horizon. Why nestle in the valley when you can frame your success with the sky?

Let me take another tack. There is a river near here that is corralled for several miles on one side by steep pine bluffs. Recently, the bluffs have become studded with so many look-at-me hill houses I am reminded of Germany's Rhine Valley and its range of cliff-topping castles. Which might give the owners of today's ersatz chateaux pause for thought, as the castles along the Rhine were stormed at fairly regular intervals. Most of the ones I've visited had been torched or shot up pretty good. Often more than once. At a time when the gulf between the haves and have-nots gapes wider yearly, the day may not be so far off when making what you "have" as obvious as a castle will be unwise. Something to ponder while sitting in your A-frame at eye level with the eagles.

Of course, all of this is little more than amateur armchair grumbling on my part. The topic cries out for a more informed opinion — the opinion, say, of a renowned landscape architect.

Now, I'm no renowned landscape architect, but I read an article

about one once. In *The New Yorker,* no less. His name was Dan Kiley.
According to the article, he was 83 years old last year, and has been
described as "the reigning classicist in landscape design." It has also
been said that he "has done more than anyone else in his field to lead
American landscape architecture back to its classical roots: to formal
geometry; to the axis, the allee, the bosquet, the terrace, the *tapis vert...*"

I wouldn't know *tapis vert* from Diet Squirt, but I do know ugly
when I see it, and so, when I saw the boat house, I fired a letter off to
Mr. Kiley. Can you spare me a note, I asked, detailing your thoughts
about this disturbing trend? I would love, I wrote, to compare my reaction (no doubt a sort of visceral parochial protectionism on my part)
to your more artistically and professionally informed opinion.

And I'll be darned if he didn't write back. A one-paragraph note,
but it did my farmboy heart good:

Office of Dan Kiley
Landscape Architects and Planners
20 November 1995

Dear Michael Perry:
It does not take an esoteric professional to explain the observation
that you make. Simply stated, people are disconnected from the land;
there is no tradition to guide them to do the right thing by the land.
Inappropriate and insensitive developments are not restricted to coun-
try areas, they are also found in the suburbs and cities.

Sincerely,
Dan Kiley

And so, my amateur grumblings validated, I feel bold enough to issue the following appeal (I don't mean to speak for Mr. Kiley, but I reckon we are in agreement on this): If the American free enterprise system has been good to you, by all means build yourself a dream house with all the doo-dads. I'm all for that. But do Dan and me a favor:

Stick it *behind* a hill.

FIGHTING FIRE

This one's for the NAAFD and all the hose we've rolled.

This morning as I slept, a man leapt from bed and jumped from the balcony of his house. Crashing to the wooden deck below, he ruptured a vertebral disk. And yet, shot through with pain, left leg gone numb, he found his feet and ran. Ran down his darkened drive, ran down damp blacktop framed in black trees, ran for half a mile to the nearest sleeping house. Leaning into the door, he pounded and shouted and sobbed.

Shortly after I moved to this town, I stopped by the monthly fire meeting. Twelve years ago, I left town a farm boy, a good student, a fair defensive end; I was returning a long-haired writer with soft hands. When the time came to introduce myself, there was foot shuffling, tipping back of chairs. Caps were adjusted. My name was penciled in the minutes. And then it was on to new business: discussion of the upcoming pig roast (barbecue versus sloppy joe), a motion to approach the fire board regarding the purchase of suspenders and a hose coupler. These things having been dealt with, the meeting was adjourned. The chief motioned me into the fire garage. He is a stout man, burly but friendly. By day he dispatches freight trucks. "Try on these boots," he said. "We've got a helmet around here somewhere." A farmer in a bar jacket showed me how to shift the pumper, his cigarette a singalong dot, dancing from word to word.

This is a tiny town — 485 souls. The feed mill is boarded up. Fluctuations in enrollment keep the school perpetually teetering on the brink of consolidation. Good jobs, when they are to be found, are often 30 or 40 miles away. During the day, the streets are still. It is from this shallow pool that the community must skim its firefighters, and I met the primary qualifications: I was frequently home during the day, and I had a pulse.

The local fire board does eventually require that you attend a firefighting course. The tools and terminology of firefighting — "halligans" and "pike poles," "double doughnuts" and "water hammer" — were quirky and lighthearted. The training exercises were a lark. We learned to unroll a 50-foot roll of hose by underhanding it like a bowling ball. We raced a stopwatch to see who could "gear up" most quickly. We practiced spraying figure eights, the fat three-inch hose stiff and insistent, shuddering with the power of compressed water. Once, the largest student in class — well over six feet tall, 250-pound range — let his attention lapse at the nozzle. The hose tipped him over as easily as if he had been nudged by an elephant. We had a good laugh.

An obstacle course was set up. I waited my turn swaddled from helmet to steel-toed boots in heavy turnout gear, sealed in the intimate, portable environment of the SCBA mask, that transparent barrier between toxic smoke and pink lungs, able to hear little beyond the easy huff and chuff of the respirator. I felt utterly isolated and protected, and recognized the sensation as the same I felt when, as a child, I would curl up in the darkness beneath a cardboard box fort. We crawled around the course in pairs, the backmost partner clinging to the leader's pack strap. Always partner up, never become separated, said the instructor. Gripping the strap, face down, unable to see, I tried to raise my head. The oxygen hose resisted, levering the mask from my face, breaking the seal. A rush of air hissed out around my ears. I realigned my face, and the hissing stopped. I still couldn't see. Scrabbling forward, I heard a clang. My oxygen bottle had struck the underside of a fire truck, wedging me against the floor. Blind, unable to move forward or back, swaddled in gear, I was suddenly air-hungry. The measured huff and chuff of the respirator became more insistent. Claustrophobia pressed in. Sweat leapt to my skin. The motion sensor attached to my collar began to caw. An image flashed: Flames. Heat. Dark smoke, thick as poison pudding. Wedged against the concrete, unable to see, unable to move, I suddenly understood what panic for oxygen might drive a man to do. I sucked air out of the tank faster and faster, wasting it, trying to keep up with my heartbeat. My partner wriggled free. I lost my grip on his strap. A thought presented itself, unbidden: You can die doing this.

And so now the fire phone beside my bed is ringing, jangling like a logging chain slung down a coal chute. In a motion, I jackknife and swivel to a sitting position, dropping my feet to the floor, groping the receiver. Yanking it from the cradle I hear the click and rattle of other receivers being lifted. A man's voice, hoarse and hurried: "Neighbor's got a fire out here. Dover Road. Whole house is goin'!" Receivers clatter. I jump for the light and grab socks. In a minute, I am running through the two back yards between my house and the fire hall. To the left and right, headlights swell from the fog, followed by the sound of engines, cottoned in the haze. Doors slam. There is the thudding of boots. We bottleneck at the small red door of the hall. Inside, the lights are fluorescent and bright. A large map is tacked to the wall. Two men search it, their fingers hurrying down lines and around corners. Little is said as we pull down boots, heavy jackets and pants, helmets, fire-proof hoods. Now there is yelling, as the chief, wearing sweat pants and a t-shirt, his hair awry, calls out directions, assigns trucks. I am to drive a tanker. I pitch my helmet in the tanker cab, follow it in. As I pop the air brake and jab at first gear, the pumper and a small, quick-response van just ahead of me light up and siren away into the dark.

The road to the fire is straight at first, and hilly. Ahead of me, the spinning red and white lights of the pumper and van alternately rise and descend, appearing and disappearing. Eventually, at a crossroad, their strobes glide east on a right angle. Alone in the cab, I hold the wide wheel, sort through the gears. At the small of my back, I can feel the willful momentum of 2,300 gallons of shifting water: Nine tons of mass in motion, ready to catch me goofing off, push me straight on a curve, drive me so far into the tagalders they'll have to fish me out with a rake. When it comes time to corner, I back off the accelerator, turn the wheel with both hands, hold my back straight as if I were balancing eggs on my head. As if the alignment of my spine could keep this truck from rolling over.

We arrive to angry sheets of flame roaring and snapping at the sky. A roiling column of smoke, milky-orange and luminous, foams upward into darkness. There is no hope of saving the house. We will simply do our best to contain the fire, to keep it from spreading. The others are already pulling hose and shrugging into air packs. I detach myself from the group and approach the man who jumped from the balcony. He is coughing and crying, shivering with fright. I remove my heavy jacket, drape it over his shoulders, radio for an ambulance. And then we watch, as a butcher, a grader operator, a farmer, a school teacher, a truck driver, a man who repairs and sells lawn mowers, a mother of five — all firefighters, now — lean into the bucking hoses and loose the cool water on their neighbor's home.

FIGHTING FIRE ... IN BELIZE

In Belize City, the capital of Belize, the 911 system is limited to the police. Fire and ambulance are summoned by dialling 90; even then, the caller must speak with a telephone company operator, who then calls the service. In Orange Walk Town, Chief Relton Petnett reports that many citizens report a fire by simply running to the fire station.

Most firefighting equipment is over 25 years old, and even when new equipment is obtained, political gamesmanship occasionally gets in the way of community service: A minister in search of votes commandeered a new pumper delivered from Canada and squirreled it away in a remote mountainous area, where it can hardly be driven, let alone effectively fight fire.

Just outside Belize City, the Phillip Goldson International Airport maintains its own 19-man firefighting force. Despite its name, most of the craft using the airport are small island-hoppers. Chief Fire Officer Emile Evans told me that to date, the most serious call the airport firefighters have responded to was an aborted takeoff resulting in a blown tire. The pilot based his decision to abort on indications of insufficient velocity for takeoff. The real problem? A butterfly wedged in the airspeed indicator. Evans keeps a picture of the butterfly in his desk.

Belize in January: Wherever I go, the locals grumble about the cold. After all, the mercury slipped to a chill 60 degrees this morning. I felt compelled, as so many northerners are — apparently on the same principle that motivates Aunt Maggie and Uncle Bob to outdo each other's arthritis stories — to haul out pictures of my Wisconsin home, buried to the windowsills in snow and socked in at 30 below. "Now *that's* cold," I'd say. Little did I know how I would be repaid for my misplaced thermal pride.

Tucked beneath the Yucatan peninsula, bordered to the north by Mexico, to the west and south by Guatemala, and flanked to the east by the Caribbean Sea, tiny Belize (8,867 square miles) is a subtropical country. The topography ranges from mountainous rainforests to pine savannahs to one of the longest coral reef systems in the world. Newly independent, and with a population of just over 200,000, Belize must maintain social, governmental, educational, military, and medical systems, all with resources equivalent to those of a small city. It's not an easy task.

BELIZE CITY

"First of all, we need more full-time manpower," says Henry Baizar, Chief of the Belize National Fire Service. He is standing in the office of the National Fire Service Headquarters in Belize City, where 18 full-time firefighters (in shifts of five) are responsible for a city of 60-70,000 (census counts are considered unreliable by many). Roughly 20 volunteers augment the force, but training is hard to come by. "Our second emphasis is on a system of training," says Baizar. "We're trying to establish a training institute. We'd like to train firefighters to a standard level, then send promising firefighters abroad for additional training."

Ted Smith has recently been appointed Operations Officer in Belize City, and is responsible for day-to-day operation of the fire station. He attended fire college in Ocala, Florida, and agrees that improved training is a priority. "Getting volunteer help is no problem, but it can be chaos," he says. "We're trying to refine the recruitment process to control the type of volunteer we get."

Belize was under British rule until 1981, and the Belizean fire service reflects the influence. Much of the equipment is British; trucks obtained through the U.S., Canada, and Korea have been retrofitted with English-made instantaneous couplers. Since Belizean independence, convenient access to North America has induced a gradual shift to more U.S.-based training. "The fittings are different," smiles Baizar, "but the principles are the same."

You can see all of Belize City from the observation tower of the National Fire Headquarters, and it is from this vantage point that the immensity of the challenge Baizar and Smith face can best be understood. Never intended to be a permanent settlement, Belize City was built for the timber trade in what was essentially a swamp at the mouth of Haulover Creek. The town lies at sea level, and has been flattened more than once by hurricanes. In the town center, the narrow, humid streets teem with street vendors and taxis, bicyclists and automobiles, uniformed school children, dogs, rag-tag street people and fanny pack-toting tourists. Twice a day, the famous Swing Bridge, which connects the two halves of the city, is swung open to allow the passage of watercraft; traffic comes to a snarled standstill. The city is crisscrossed by polluted canals and open sewer drains. In overpopulated poverty-stricken sections, wooden houses — many on stilts — huddle, nearly touching, along single-track lanes studded with potholes the size of cow tanks. Belize City was recently described in a guidebook as "a hazardous fire trap." It is a description Baizar understands only too well. "For a firefighter, Belize City is a nightmare," he says. "In the old part of the city, 75% of the houses are wooden. There are more than three or four buildings in each yard, with only two or three feet separating them. A fire starts, and in 20 minutes, they're flat. Most of the time, we contain. Simply ensure that it doesn't spread. In February 1993, a fire in the old part of town burned 16 houses before it was stopped. The flames jumped the streets."

Fire attack is further hampered by limited water sources. The Belize

City department responds with an E-One pumper (1250 gallon capacity) and a small Nissan pumper. A limited number of hydrants are available, and the firefighters must frequently draw water from open sewer canals. "They need to learn to regulate their pressure, combine their water sources," says Ted Smith. "Fifty p.s.i. is usually about the maximum pressure available." When drafting from the canals, a woven wicker suction attachment is used to strain the ... well, you can imagine.

Of additional concern to Baizar and Smith is an Esso refinery located on the city seashore. "At least we have lots of water there," jokes Baizar. The department works with Esso on routine exercises, and Esso owns some firefighting equipment of its own, but there is little doubt that an incident at the refinery would severely challenge the resources of the department.

In the end, "resources" means "money," and as Ted Smith says with a shake of his head, "There's never enough money." And yet, in the face of an infrastructure in its inefficient infancy, and a lack of equipment, supplies, and manpower, he spends part of the morning drilling the day crew over a map of the refinery. In the afternoon, he leads a fire safety training session at the hospital; he will do the same at a number of schools this year. Meanwhile, Baizar is working to restructure the service, make it more responsive to the unique needs of this unique country. In time, the most important firefighting Ted Smith and Henry Baizar do will be somewhere other than at the end of a hose.

ORANGE WALK TOWN

The congestion of Belize City aside, Belize is a beautiful country. During the two-hour bus ride north from Belize City to Orange Walk

Town, congested city streets give way to a piney savannah; circling frigate birds and pelicans give way to snowy egrets and the occasional cow. Orange Walk Town (pop. 12,000) has the feel of a frontier border town. Buses from Mexico pass through town nearly nonstop. Large trucks loaded with sugar cane roar down the main street 'round the clock, headed for the giant sugar refinery just to the south. People on the streets are quick to smile, and the cane haulers offer a ride to anyone who waves a hand.

From his vantage point near the town center, Fire Chief Relton Petnett has a constant sense of the rhythm of the town. An informally friendly man, he lives in a house attached to the station, and can generally be found framed in one of the open bay doors seven days a week. Formerly with the Belize City force, he didn't think he'd like his Orange Walk assignment. "Life is much slower here," he says, grinning. "But now I like it."

Firefighting in the Orange Walk district is often related to the sugar industry. "The farmers burn the cane in the field prior to harvest, and the fire can get away," says Petnett. "As a result, we get a lot of bush fires — wildfires. We also have a large sawmill nearby. The wildfires in the savannah move to the sawmill and hit the sawdust. The fire burns beneath the sawdust. You soak it, and ten minutes later there's smoke coming out of the ground again. We've taken to using a backhoe, digging a trench ahead of the fire line and filling it with water. We also do a lot of backburns, letting fire fight fire."

Petnett and his small crew have two vehicles at their disposal: a 250-gallon Carmichael attack vehicle, and a 25-year-old, 1100-gallon Dennis tanker. A siren summons volunteer firefighters when necessary, and Petnett has rigged his own communication center using a car radio and assorted parts. "It can be frustrating up here," he says. "It takes a long, long time for parts and equipment to arrive. It can take three months to get a dry powder extinguisher filled. In many cases, if you want something done, you end up doing it yourself." He gestures at his homemade communication center and grins. "No computers, like the U.S.A.!"

BELMOPAN

In 1961, after yet another hurricane thrashed Belize City, the government decided to move the capital inland. In the end, it was hoped, the citizenry would follow, and this new city, Belmopan, would become the cultural and commercial center of the country. There was just one problem — they built the capital, but no one came. Today, less than 4,000 people inhabit the city. And so it is that the entire fire department for the Belizean equivalent of Washington, D.C., can be found in a one-vehicle garage at the edge of town. Chief Ernest "Mark" Dominguez can see the capitol from the front door of his house — which is next door to his one fire truck. Much of the countryside surrounding Belmopan is dry and piney; as a result, many of Dominguez's calls are made outside the capital. "I have had wildfire suppression training, which has been very helpful," he says. He has also had EMT training, and responds to motor vehicle accidents in the area; his Carmichael is outfitted for extrication with an air chisel and a jigsaw.

SAN IGNACIO

Twelve miles from the Guatemalan border, the San Ignacio fire station perches high above the banks of Garbutt Creek. The station has no radio, but from where the requisite Carmichael attack vehicle and aged

Dennis tanker are parked, the firemen can see most of the picturesque town for which they are responsible. Fidel Castanedez is inside the cool garage, filling out training logs. I mention a word, and he grins. Belizean firefighters may be struggling to establish and formalize their profession, but they are already familiar with that one universal byproduct of organization: *paperwork.*

HOME

I stopped by the fire hall when I got home. We have 485 residents in this town, and yet, our two pumpers, three tankers, one rescue van, and one brush buggy leave us more amply equipped than Belize City and its thousands. We are fortunate.

I discovered upon my return that temperatures had consistently occupied the 50-below range during my absence. This troubled me, as it meant I had been wasting 20 degrees of thermal bragging rights in Belize. Then I went to my basement and discovered even more thermal bragging rights: a burst pipe. Standing in six inches of water, watching it cascade from the crack and ricochet off the wall, I thought of Ted Smith and Henry Baizar, and grinned. They might not care for this weather, but think what they could do with this kind of water pressure!

STEVE EARLE, HARD-CORE TROUBADOR

Before you read this piece you need to know some things:

❖ *Steve Earle has been married six times.*
❖ *Steve Earle has poor driving habits.*
❖ *Steve Earle took a break from the making of music through the mid-1990s in order that he might increase his consumption of regrettable substances, live in real bad parts of town, and break a few traffic laws. Then he had a nice rest in jail.*
❖ *Steve Earle is bigger than I and has more tattoos.*
❖ *Steve Earle wrote and recorded "My Old Friend The Blues" long before the Proclaimers were proclaiming.*
❖ *Steve Earle sings country music without the aid of a Stetson, a belt buckle or a cute little butt.*
❖ *Steve Earle is the real deal.*
❖ *I like Steve Earle. Of course I've never had to ride with him. Or marry him.*

Cadott, Wisconsin, 1994. Country Fest. Notebook in hand, I stand in darkness as six lovely boys who missed the White Lion reunion tour casting call get 30,000 drunken cheeseheads in a cow pasture to hoist their thirty-fifth beer of the day to the night sky and scream "God Blessed Texas!" It occurs to me that something is drastically wrong.

Geneva, Switzerland. April 27, 1996. Country Jamboree at the Palexpo. I was warned, and it's true: many Swiss country music fans show up dressed in period clothing, including toy pistols, sheriff's badges and even a headdress or two. As a Confederate general prices felt cowboy hats in the lobby, his petticoated daughter stumbles over his dangling sabre.

Cannock, England. April 30, 1996. Since I was here last, seven years have passed. The coal mines have shut down. The surrounding farmland has disappeared under a mitotic profusion of two-story brick duplexes; meadow and gorse have been subdivided by tarmac strips dubbed Meadow Way and Gorse Lane. The traffic circles are jammed with young professionals fleeing the decay of nearby Birmingham, but crime is hitching a ride. The town council responded by filling the old town center with tulips, bandstand gazebos and cobblestoned doses of "quaint." Still, the council is under pressure to do more: Surveillance cameras — "like the ones in Birmingham" — are on order. And then, the bad news: While hiding out over coffee and a buttered scone at George and Bertie's Tea Room — one of Cannock's surviving links to the past — I hear the waitress tell the cook about her plans for Friday night: American line-dancing lessons. Seems it's the rage in England at the moment. And to think they're all worked up about Mad Cow Disease.

The day I left England for Switzerland, my English friend Tim rose early to take me to the train, leaving him no time to make his usual two sandwiches. And so, at lunch, he went to a greasy truck stop near his work site. A big ugly trucker was just finishing his chips; Tim asked if he could have the trucker's newspaper. The trucker grunted and pushed it Tim's way. Somewhere in the middle-of-nowhere pages, a tiny concert notice caught his eye. Steve Earle and the Dukes, Birmingham Town Hall. Having endured my raves about an Earle show I'd seen in March, he got on the phone immediately and secured a set of tickets.

I knew nothing of this as I walked home from George and Bertie's, heavy laden with thoughts of how the Nashvirus, no longer confined to U.S. cow pastures, has infected Boot-Scootin' Brits and Swiss cowpokes. When Tim called, he asked if I'd be interested in seeing a band called the Dukes, with some guy named Steve Earle. The wry British sense of humor, you understand. He picked me up at six, and we headed for Birmingham, against the nocturnal flow of subdivision-bound escapees.

Birmingham, England. The Town Hall looks more like the Parthenon than a town hall. Steve Earle lumbers onstage and renders the point moot: within six bars of "Feel Alright," the joint's a roadhouse. Next, he rocks through "Hard-Core Troubador," and further stomps all over the notion that rehab and living in Nashville may have deadened his muse. Indeed, each of the eleven songs he performed from the twelve-song *I Feel Alright* album (the second since his infamous "vacation in the ghetto") stand as proof of his artistic survival. His penchant for diplomacy has survived, as well: Explaining why none of the *I Feel Alright* songs will be released as a single in England, he quips, "It's because...well, it's because we're sick of kissin' [BBC] Radio One's ass." Cheers all around. Curmudgeonry is replaced with a twinkling eye, however, when he grins over the opening chords of "My Old Friend the Blues," and says, "Here's an old Proclaimers song."

Midway through the show, the Dukes vacate the stage, leaving Earle to solo with an acoustic guitar and harmonica. As he did in Minneapolis, Earle performs "State Trooper," from Bruce Springsteen's *Nebraska*, introducing it as a song written by "a hillbilly from New Jersey." He introduces "Valentine's Day" with the humorous tale of how the song came about as a result of his being legally deprived of the right to drive. Earle's habit of bracketing lyric lines with audible breaths is powerfully emotive in an acoustic setting; during "Ellis Unit One," written for *Dead Man Walking,* the effect is positively chilling.

As the Dukes rejoin him, Earle tunes up for "Billy and Bonnie." "How y'all doin'?" he asks the crowd. A few "alrights" are heard, but from my darkened back row balcony seat, your humble reviewer inexplicably bellers, "ALL THE WAY FROM WISCONSIN, MAN!" Earle stops dead. "Wisconsin! Damn!" Next, I devolve completely from objective concert critic to blatant panty-tossing teenie-bopper fan mode: "WOOOOOO!!!!" Earle plays the opening riff, then stops again. "Wisconsin! I thought I was a long way from home. Man, you're lost!" By this time humiliation and the fear of being beat up by the main attraction has enabled me to shut up. The rest of the show is like blastin' down a backroad in a badass hot rod; things just keep gettin' faster and louder. By the time we scream into "Guitar Town," the English have stormed the stage, and my buddy Tim has sung himself hoarse. I find myself desperately wishing all those Little Texas fans could be here. I want to fly in the Swiss family Confederate, get them vaccinated against the Nashvirus for life. I want that tea room waitress next to me pistoning her fist to "Copperhead Road," thoroughly purged of the need to ever again hook her thumbs in her belt loops.

But nothing's worse than a proselytizer; they gotta get it on their own. So until they do, lemme preach to the choir: The coal mines are gone, but Steve Earle is back. Lordy, is he back. Makes me wanna holler.

THE MOON BRINGS NOT PLEASURE

First, I must thank my mother the archivist; she preserved this bit of history and passed it on to me.

One-and-a-quarter centuries after my great-great-great-grandfather died, I learned of his death at war from a letter written by his young wife. The scenes which follow were created from clues left in that letter; the quotes from that letter are verbatim.

For those who wait at home, war has its own special cruelty.

Framed in a square of moonlight, Matilda Root stands silent in the bedroom of her children. The night is warm, and still. There is no sound save the peaceful rhythm of the children's breathing. The moonlight seeps from her shoulders to her feet before Matilda leaves the room.

In the kitchen, Matilda strikes a match. The rasp of the stroke and the hiss of burning sulfur fill the room. Touching the match to the wick of a hurricane lamp, Matilda waits until the flame has taken hold before replacing the fluted chimney. Light shudders across the walls.

From a flat wooden box beside the lamp, Matilda removes a few sheaves of paper, a pen, and a small jar of ink. She arranges a sheet of paper before her, readies the pen, and begins to write:

Haney Valley, July 3rd, 1865

Dear Sister:

I will try this pleasant evening to communicate my thoughts to you through the medium of a silent pen, but Oh! bad thoughts indeed they are to me. The evening is indeed very pleasant; the moon looks forth smilingly upon the earth, but it brings not pleasure to me.

The script is feminine and strong, the strokes bold and composed.

> *To think that I am left sad and lonely, my poor dear companion sleep-*
> *ing in the dust, his soul I trust is at peace with God which is a great*
> *consolation to us yet it is heart rending to think we shall never meet*
> *more on earth, to think he suffered so many privations and was just*
> *anticipating being at home...*

Matilda puts the pen aside. Reaching into the wooden box, she draws out a small envelope, dark with fingerprints. On the back of the envelope are the words, "Merit H. Root, Co. C., 49 Reg Wis Vol, via Nashville Tenn." The letter within the envelope is thin, its creases sharp and beginning to tear. Matilda unfolds it gently, caressing it to flatness on the table. She looks at the letter for a very long time, never seeing the words.

Merit H. Root was 25 years old.

> *...it makes my heart ache to think of all these things yet we have to*
> *view stern reality and submit to the will of a just and holy God. Oh!*
> *sister I wish I could see you at this time we could sympathise with*
> *each other in this hour of affliction and distress as Mercy and Lucy*
> *have bothe written to you since we heard the painful news of Merit's*
> *death.*

Matilda pauses to immerse the tip of the pen in the ink once more. She draws a long breath. As it flows from her body, she begins to write again.

Oh! sister he had talked and thought much about coming out there
on a visit, but now alas! you will meet no more untill you meet at the
judgement seat Oh! may we all meet there to part no more where
sickness, sorrow, pain and death are felt and feared no more; where I
trust that Merit dear boy is singing the song of redeeming love...

The cleft blade of the pen scratches across the parchment roughly,
faintly.

I rec'd your picture and thank you very much for it. I must bid you
good night for the present. Please write soon Oh! it is so lonely not to
receive letters from dear Merit any more. Please write very soon.
Good by.

M E Root

The letter is left to dry, the lamp extinguished. Pausing to look at
her children once more, Matilda stands now in darkness, the moon
obscured. The children breathe evenly. The rhythm is unchanged.

In her tiny bedroom across the short hallway, Matilda can still hear
the children. She undresses without light, exchanging her blouse and
long skirt for a plain nightdress. Dipping to her knees, she begins a
long, silent prayer.

Once in bed, Matilda begins to breathe in the rhythm of her children. Her hand strays to the pillow beside her own.

AARON TIPPIN:
A HOLLER FULL OF TRUCKS

A ways east of Nashville, there's a holler full of trucks. Eleven of 'em, a rough, beat-up bunch, faced inward on a semicircle. At one end of that semicircle is an old wooden shop. You can read a lot about a man by his shop. This one is generally organized, but retains the comfortable clutter of use. A worn stand-up toolbox stands front and center; a screwdriver handle and a few wrenches protrude from gapped drawers. A torn-down transfer case rests alongside a homemade straddle pit. There's an old yellow fridge covered in stickers, a plumb ugly bench upholstered in naugahyde, a tiny, tinny boom box tuned to a country station, and a pair of dusty fishing poles. And hung on a hook on one wall, along with a mess of other things, an old forest green hard hat. On the side, in scuffed orange letters, it says, "98 TIP."

"TIP" is Aaron Tippin, the man who first caught the attention of country music fans in 1991 with the single, "You've Got To Stand For Something." Other hits followed —"Workin' Man's Ph.D.," "I Wouldn't Have It Any Other Way," and "My Blue Angel." Since his debut hit, Tippin has produced three gold albums, one platinum album, and is currently on the charts with his fifth and most recent album, "Tool Box." Not bad. But today we don't spend five minutes talking about music. Aaron Tippin wants to talk about his trucks.

Tippin's trucks aren't museum pieces. He's pulled them out of junkyards, yanked them from the weeds, even spotted a few along America's backroads from the window of his tour bus. But where did it all begin? "I think it was kind of an accident," chuckles Tippin. He points across the clearing where his former bus driver, Smitty, is carving out a pad for a bus garage, moving fill with a red and black '74 Ford F750. "First dump truck I had on the place," he says. "It's been a good old truck. But I got it, and I thought, this thing won't hold enough dirt to suit me, so I found that old Mack over there." Tippin nods toward a Mack B42 at the far end of the row. It has a black box, and a cab best described as "yaller." "Bought it over in Dixon, Tennessee. Me and Smitty went out there and got it cranked, got it goin', and away we went. It had dirty old fuel in it — I mean the fuel was like motor oil, and it was still runnin'! But it kept gettin' slower and slower, so we stopped and put a new fuel filter in it, and POW! She took off like a shot.

"That's the funny thing about these old Macks. Generally, if they're sittin', in any condition similar to this, you hook a chain to'em and in twenty feet, they're runnin'. They wanna live more'n anything I've ever been around." Tippin's eyes are bright. "Now that is a spectacular feelin'. Tuggin' on an ol' truck, seein' that smoke comin' outta the stack, then she cracks, and then BRROOOM, it comes to life, and everybody that's helpin' can't help but dance around and holler a little bit."

Tippin points out a Mack B61 dump truck. "This one's special. I got that from a good friend, Billy Ferguson. Billy did the whole campaign with Patton in World War II...talk about stories! The Ferguson brothers got out of the war, came home and bought a dump truck. And now anybody in Mississippi knows the Ferguson Brothers company. They still run Macks."

Next in line is a faded red Mack tractor. "That's an LJ," says Tippin. "I believe it's a '47. The cab is built on a wood frame. It's got a Cummins engine in it, which is unusual for a Mack. They tell me that's one of the first over the road trucks built that'd do a hundred mile an hour. Buddy, that's flyin'!" Next to the LJ, a Mack B67 is hooked to a lowboy. "I bought that off a guy in Missouri. It was out there rustin' away. That's an old 40-ton two-axle lowboy. Forty tons on two axles is unheard of nowadays. I use it to haul my dozer."

The other trucks in the semicircle include a '61 White Mustang in-line six-cylinder gas burner with a short dump box, and a pair of Mack H67 cabovers. "I figure I'd like to get me a cabover goin'," says Tippin. "If you're gonna haul equipment in tight places, you're better off with a short wheelbase, and you can see a little better outta that thing, too."

Tippin has been using his trucks (and a small fleet of excavation equipment) to complete several major projects on his farm, including the bus garage, a driveway that winds through the hills like a dusty Cumberland River, a clearing and basement for his new house, and soon, a runway. "In the end, I'd like to restore one or two of'em," says Tippin, "but until we get done what we need done, they gotta work."

Tippin's love for working trucks was born early. "Six years old, growin' up on the farm, I was too little to carry a bale of hay, so I got the steerin' wheel of the truck. Dad put'er in gear and she'd idle down through the field at 3 mile an hour and you just kept'er straight."

Tippin's father was also a flier, and the youngster fell in love with airplanes. He got a pilot's license and was steering toward a career as a commercial pilot when the 1980s' energy crisis led to his being laid off and grounded his plans. And so, still in his early 20s, Tippin got his CDL. "I pulled for Cooper Motor Lines. Drove a White Road Commander. Then I drove a Jimmy for Carolina Western, haulin' dry freight." Between runs he took up serious bodybuilding and started playing honky-tonks, but the days when he would see his songs in the charts were still years away. So he kept working, accumulating experiences that influence his music to this day.

The bright lights have done little to fade the blue from his collar. When I ask him about the old green hard hat hanging in the shop, his voice drops, becomes almost reverent. "That's my old construction hat. Sure is. That's the real deal." Tippin wore the helmet during years spent welding bridge girders and stainless steel textile mill equipment. Nowadays he dons a hard hat to open his shows. "Someone told me I should use my old construction hat, and I said, `No, that hat ain't for fun. It's for real.'"

This topic brings about a moment of truth: I once wrote in a review that the hard hat reminded me of long-lost novelty act The Village People. I tell Tippin so. It's not a comfortable moment, facing someone you've criticized in print, but after a short pause (seemed long to me), Tippin chuckles. "Yeah, that's why I wear it for one song and then get it off!" But then the grin fades, and he looks me straight in the eye. "I've been whupped and whupped by people who write stories about how corny it is, but obviously, to the crowd, it's not corny. I do "Workin' Man's Ph.D.," or "I Got It Honest," and they're on their feet. They get it the same way I feel it. That's important to me...that's who I'm tryin' to please."

Tippin's CDL is still current, and comes in handy when he and his band are on the road. "Buses now have to abide by the same laws as the trucks do, as far as drivin' hours are concerned. Generally if we have an overdrive somewhere, I drive...so it depends where we've got to go. If it's California, I've got a leg in it somewhere."

But from farm trucks to tour buses, you can bet he'd rather be jamming a set of old gears. "I always loved the old B trucks," says Tippin. "When I was in excavation, I worked for a guy who had one. It had two shifters...you had to *drive* this truck. We meet a lot of drivers when we're on the road, and I guarantee you, if an old B model Mack pulls into a truck stop, every driver there goes and takes a look at it, because..." Tippin pauses, nods his camouflage cap toward his half-circle of old rubber and steel, ready to rattle to life and lug a load. "...Because it's out there still doin' what it was born to do."

HIRSUTE PURSUITS

Despite what this piece says, I'm not 28 anymore. I'm also still a ways from bald. But things ain't gettin' any thicker.

Over ten years ago, while clambering over an oil drilling rig, I fell headlong down a flight of 25 steel steps and knocked myself unconscious. While I sustained no long term damage, the event was marked by a small scar just inside my hairline.

Recently, while peering in the mirror, I made a relevatory discovery: for future retellings of the "I-fell-off-an-oil-rig" story, it is no longer necessary that I part my hair to reveal the scar which verifies the tale.

Yep, at the relatively tender age of 28, it has become clear that I am losing the hair war. For nearly a quarter of a century, my scalp was protected by rank legions of hair. Then came the thinning of the ranks — followed by a general retreat from the front. These days, I don't so much comb my hair as harvest it — can complete surrender be far behind?

Bald. The word itself drops flat and ugly from the tongue. It has no bounce, no redeeming phonic personality. Worse yet, it is employed in the description of items past their useful life; i.e., tires and old carpet. A simple lie becomes an outrageous prevarication when characterized as "bald-faced." Even its association with the regal fowl symbolic of our great nation has failed to lend any dignity to this monosyllabic utterance.

Ahh, but never has there been a better time to go bald...after all, this is the age of the infomercial, and for my money, nothing is more amusing than a rollicking half hour of hair replacement therapy (which usually features a celebrity whose hairline and career are both in a state of recess). Just try to beat the entertainment value of watching a rather delicate gentleman "thickening" hair with sprinkles of colored powder from what appears to be a pepper shaker. Lots of on-cue oohing and aahing occurs, and each sprinkle is accompanied by a series of dainty "pats" on the head. As entertaining as this is, it's not for me. I'd probably show up at parties looking as if I were afflicted with brown dandruff. Furthermore, I don't fancy spending a lot of time patting myself.

In another infomercial, a fast-talking gent spraypaints bald spots, racing gleefully from from pate to pate, insisting all the while that he's not spraypainting. Again, a lot of patting is involved, and despite strategically lit "before and after" pictures, a little voice inside my head continues to suggest that the emperor has no hair.

Then there's the one where an earnest trio of folks in expensive clothing offer to relocate chunks of the hair you have *left* into the places your hair left *from*. Seems a little too much like gardening to me. Yet another company actually weaves *faux* hair into place. Weaving: Isn't that how they make rugs?

A major pharmaceutical company offers a hair-sprouting ointment that actually works, with two qualifications: don't expect hair like Fabio; do expect a monthly pharmacy bill the size of Fabio's pecs.

And so, short of getting sprinkled, sprayed, plugged, woven, or refinanced, what is a balding man to?

Support groups are available, but who wants to sit around moaning about hair loss with a bunch of bald guys? If I need someone to hold my hand while I go bald, what will happen when I start to get liver spots, or develop an arthritic thumb? No thanks, I shall call upon my reserves of Scandinavian stoicism and tough this one out on my own.

I suppose I could start wearing hats. I have noticed that a certain famous country music star (who is able, with a simple twist of the hips, to reduce groups of normally well-behaved women to screaming throngs of lingerie-tossing fanatics) is more likely to whistle a medley of Barry Manilow jingles than remove his Stetson in public. Methinks he is keeping something (or nothing) under his hat.

But I'm not really a hat guy. Oh, they're nice — and if I thought by wearing one I could reduce groups of normally well-behaved women to screaming throngs of lingerie-tossing fanatics, I might give it a shot — but I've never really gotten used to them. For one thing, when I played football, I had the biggest helmet on the team. When we were measured for our high school graduation caps, yours truly topped the circumference list. Same story in college. So finding headgear that fits comfortably is a challenge. Adjustable caps offer an option, but most of these are emblazoned with team logos or mildly profane aphorisms...not my style.

And so, as my forehead continues to expand (leaving me to savor the scintillating humor inherent in statements the likes of, "Say there Mac, yer forehead's turnin' into a *five*head, yuk, yuk"), I think I'll just get on with life. After all, it's not as if something really critical were falling out — like my pancreas, for instance.

As in nearly all things, if you look hard enough, there is a bright spot to be found amidst all this hair loss. Unfortunately, it happens to be the reflection of my bathroom light.

STEVE GUNDERSON
AND THE GAME OF POLITICS

Kevin Kennedy has a voice designed to smooth your lapels. Right now he is apologizing. It's time for a scheduled interview with his boss, Congressman Steve Gunderson, and Gunderson is not to be found. "I think Steve had to go to the floor for a vote," he says in the professionally regretful tones of a funeral director offering his deepest sympathies on the death of your dear Aunt Rose. It was Rose, wasn't it?

Modulating his voice with all the care of a deejay spinning the lite hits of the '70s, Kennedy informs me that he must put me on hold while he verifies the location of his boss. The congressional on-hold experience is a good-old-fashioned silent one. Mercifully free of the lite hits of the '70s.

Soon he is back. "I guess Steve *is* here, Mike! Hang on for just a minute and he'll be with you!" I feel as if I am the tenth caller. The lucky listener. I won the tickets. Kevin signs off. Steve signs on.

I have no bones to pick with Steve Gunderson. My assignment is to deliver a profile of the man, not hammer any specific issue. Nonetheless, I am determined to let him know that I do not intend to subject my readers to rehashed soundbites.

"I want to avoid canned answers, congressman," I say in my best "take charge" tone. Gunderson chuckles. "That's your problem, not mine!" Of course he's dead right. Were I a baseball pitcher, this exchange would be the equivalent of the leadoff hitter rapping my first pitch for a single. So much for throwing high and tight. I lob a run-of-the-mill personal history question.

"I'm a small-town boy," says Gunderson. Born in 1951 and elected to the Wisconsin State Assembly in 1974, he describes himself as a young, scared kid from Pleasantville, Wisconsin, who ran as a Republican at the height of Watergate-induced anti-Republican sentiment because "I feared for the safety of the two-party system." The fact that Gunderson has recently benefitted from a pro-Republican shift has only given rise to new concerns about that system.

"The worst of what is happening now is that partisan polarization is feeding the politics of personal destruction. The Republicans are consumed with destroying Bill and Hillary Clinton personally. The Democrats are consumed with destroying Newt Gingrich personally. Not because of their policies; we're not trying to debate issues, to prove whether Hillary Clinton is right or wrong on health care, we're trying to make her out as a slut. I mean, it just boggles my mind. And the Democrats are not trying to disagree with The Contract, they're trying to make Newt Gingrich out as a crook. Where do we come from!?!" (For the record, this writer had the impression that it was Bill everyone was trying to make out as a...well, you know.)

Concerns about this polarization drove Gunderson to decry the 1992 Republican convention, and more recently, his fears that a "hard-right" shift in the leadership did not reflect the Republican mainstream drove him to step down from his position as chief deputy minority whip. The decision to step down was more than symbolic, according to Gunderson. "I felt after '92 the Republican party needed some visible presence in the ideological center, and that it was not being offered by others. My role in the whip organization precluded me really from doing that — I had to be more of a team player than a spokesman.

"I think we are in power now not because we are the right, the center or the left, but we are in power now for two reasons. Number one, there was a very anti-Washington message sent in the '94 elections. We should not kid ourselves; Bill Clinton helped us a great deal in that regard. But second, I think we did not scare the public in '94 like we did in '92. In '92 we were perceived as a party of intolerance and a party of exclusion. That message was not a part of 1994."

For years, the issue of Gunderson's homosexuality was the subject of speculation and murmur; more recently it has been the source of several news stories, and, during the '94 campaigns, a brief spate of heavy-handed commercials that revealed more about the character of his minor party opponent than about Gunderson. Apparently determined to fend off pressure to be a "poster boy" for either the left or right, Gunderson was quoted in a pre-election article in the Advocate, saying, "I'm not running for re-election to advance the gay cause. The reasons I'm running are the issues that happen to be very important to my district — the farm bill, passing and implementing a health care bill and supporting vocational education." When addressing gay and lesbian organizations, Gunderson has both acknowledged his homosexuality and defended conservative colleagues, including Newt Gingrich. "I tell them they need to understand that anti-government doesn't mean anti-gay."

The fifteen minutes I have been allotted for the telephone interview are nearly spent. I ask Gunderson what he intends to do when his current (and — he says — his last) term in Congress expires.

"I honestly don't know." he says. "I'd like to start a business, I'd like to teach, I'd like to write a book about the politics of polarization, but I really don't know." Part of the territory that comes with being a long-time politician is that writers don't always believe you when you say things like "I honestly don't know," and so I press the question. My indefatigable determination is rewarded when Gunderson chuckles and reveals, "Well, I do know that whatever I do, I don't want to spend January in Wisconsin."

Now there's a man speaking the truth.

In the days to follow, I have several more phone conversations with the solicitous Kevin Kennedy. I am attempting to set up a face-to-face interview with the congressman. I soon learn that with Mr. Kennedy, initiative is rewarded (read: the squeaky wheel....). "Yes, I was just about to call you," he intones, sounding for all the world as if he was. Of course, my inferences are disingenuous. It's not as if I expect him to answer the phone with a hearty "'yallo!" His polished demeanor is remarkable in the face of the ceaseless cascade of complaints and requests he must face daily. And when I arrived to perform the face-to-face interview at a "town meeting" in the small town of Barron, Wisconsin, I found everything arranged as promised, down to the last detail. So despite my backwoods predilection to take cheap shots at cultivated manners and diction, here's to Kevin Kennedy; he delivered as promised.

The day of the town meeting arrives. Constituents begin trickling in thirty minutes before Gunderson is due to speak. Many clutch notebooks. Most are gray-haired, and several descend the sloping auditorium floor with the rocking gait of "farmer's hip." The level of conversation swells in congruence with the size of the crowd. Occasionally an exchange rises above the murmur.

"You gonna talk?"

"I don't know yet..."

"Did you talk before the county board ever?"

"Hey, c'mere Bud! Sit up front — your ears ain't that good!"

Gunderson approaches through a hallway. After 21 years in public office he is a master of the on-the-move "meet and greet." Soon he is at the front of the auditorium, arranging folding chairs and bantering with a group of older men who look as if they came straight from their daily coffee and doughnut summit.

The congressman opens the meeting with a wide-ranging mono-logue on current issues, from per-child tax credits to term limits. The bulk of the introduction focuses on balancing the budget.

"I don't say this with any kind of satisfaction, but I am not sure this country is ready for the steps that are required to balance the bud-get. I think it is going to require a test of commitment, of courage and hopefully fairness from all of us that I am not sure that we are ready to commit to."

He is equally frank about the prospects of bipartisan cooperation. "You should expect some gridlock in Washington come fall. I think that the one most disappointing thing I've seen so far is literally no attempt by the leadership of either party to figure out how to work out some bipartisan discussions to get things done. And I'll be critical of both sides on that.

"The likelihood of the federal government shutting down a few times [in October, when the new fiscal year begins] is probably pretty good because there simply won't be a funding resolution to fund it."

After the monologue, Gunderson opens the floor for questions. He lists three specific ground rules, the last of which is, "If you don't swear at me, I won't swear at you."

The questions are diverse, ranging from school lunch to vocational education. Many of the individuals read their questions from notes. For nearly two hours, a relaxed Gunderson replies to each question specifically and at length, often while leaning back against a table, arms crossed. As when he is being interviewed, his answers come quickly, without hesitation. A gifted political animal, he is smooth and well-rehearsed, but his answers are thorough and specific. Whether his ques-tioners agree or disagree with his response, the town meeting setting provides a welcome respite from the sound bite.

A man from Cumberland, Wisconsin, rises to his feet, expressing concern about proposed tax cuts in the face of a deficit. Grinning, Gunderson reveals that he may work in Washington, but he pays attention to noises from the nooks and crannies of home. "I can't help but suggest that if you're from Cumberland you must have been reading the editorial in the Cumberland paper this past week!" The room chuckles.

Another man, not content with Gunderson's response to his question, wants to argue the point. Gunderson engages him politely, directly and firmly. "No. This clearly would be prohibited by the regulatory moratorium. No question about it. Next question." The man settles into his seat with a quick waggle of his head, unconvinced. Later, he leaves the session early.

In response to an inquiry about the well-publicized parking lot "perk" at Washington National Airport, Gunderson surprises some in attendance by defending the lot. "Folks, the alternative is to pay [the regular rates] for the parking at National Airport [and get reimbursed for those expenses]."

Only once does Gunderson seem caught unprepared. "What kind of influence do you have with the Coast Guard?" says a man in a high-pitched voice, the jut of his chin nearly intersecting with the forward tilt of his greasy baseball hat. "Weelll..." says Gunderson, "I haven't *tried* to have any influence with them, so I don't know!" It turns out the man's concerns have to do with life preservers. "I'm terribly upset that the government deems it their job to tell me what I have to do in my boat," he says, taking his seat. An elderly woman one seat ahead of me frowns in his direction. "It's only for your own good," she mutters.

Gunderson wraps up the meeting with another brief monologue. As the last of the crowd filters out, he discusses the town meeting concept. "There has to be this kind of dialogue so that even if people disagree with me on an issue they do not dislike me. I've got to win the personality contest before I have any hope of winning the ideological discussion. Also, the worst fear I have is that people think I would take advantage of these last two years of congress as a luxury ride where I would not serve my constituents. I want people to look back on my service and say 'we've never had a harder-working congressman.' Not somebody who says, 'in his last term he forgot where home was.'"

I ask the congressman what he thinks of the popularity of talk radio. His answer is quick and unequivocal. "Oh, I think it's harmful. It could be very helpful, because clearly the public's more educated than they've ever been. The problem is that the success of talk radio is based on the cynicism and polarization that it produces. And I think that that is not helpful in a democratic society." As a tenacious journalist, I should have asked him if he didn't agree, however, that as a Republican, it is kind of handy to have Rush Limbaugh plugging the Contract with America five days per week, eh? But I didn't think of that rapier retort until just now. I know Mike Wallace, and I'm no Mike Wallace.

Gunderson eyes the clock. He is due in the Twin Cities. I ask him what it's like to be leaving the game with his team winning. "Oh, it's absolutely wonderful. I mean, the fact that you can go out at the top, you can go out when you're not burned out, you can go out when you are at the peak of your energy and your influence, I think that is a wonderful way to end a congressional career — but more important, I would hope that people would say that it also shows that Steve was not consumed by it. I don't think anyone can accuse me of having Potomac fever or being drunk with power or being consumed by politics. I love my job, I love the work, but I understand that there's much more to life than just politics."

As we walk to the small red car in which he will be driven to the Cities, I ask him once more what his post-Congress plans are. He smiles. "I really don't know."

"Does the term 'cabinet member' mean anything to you?" I ask.

"Get outta here," he laughs, climbing into the passenger seat. The car pulls away from the sidewalk, rounds a corner, and disappears over a hill. Steve Gunderson is on the move.

Postscript:
Since I wrote this profile, Gunderson and his partner Rob Morris have published the memoir House and Home.

Gunderson's comments about the government shutdown were prescient; his comments about "going out at the top" may be tempered somewhat by the elections of 1996. Time will tell.

Dare I say this in print? Contrary to every instinct I possess regarding politicians, I admire Steve Gunderson. So many politicians, blinkered in the immobilizing grip of ideology, reduce themselves to impotent ranters, convinced the journey to truth is accomplished only through the repetitive, shrill yammering of party line sound bites. Steve Gunderson dared to suggest (and then hang around to illustrate) that issues were rarely clearcut; in the latter days of his career, elements of both the political left and political right sought to spin the image of an openly gay Republican congressman to their advantage. Not only did Gunderson rebuff these advances, he openly rebuked those intent on obscuring his service with his personhood.

LIFE IN THE FAT LANE

I knew writing an article like this without upsetting someone would be a tricky proposition. Several months after it hit print, I was at a family reunion. One of my aunts, whose metabolism is stacked against her, approached me. "I saw your 'fat' article when I was checking out at the grocery store," she said. "I had to buy the magazine to see just what you had to say." I looked at her like a cornered dog who spots someone approaching with a rolled-up newspaper.

"I think you did all right," she smiled. "It didn't seem like you were picking on anyone."

I began to breathe again. Never mind literary critics in ivory towers. It's aunts at reunions who can cut your career short.

You look like you've put on some weight.

Think I'm rude? Insensitive? Sorry, but the experts and their numbers back me up. Diane Dresel is the Coordinator of Health Management Resources at Midelfort Clinic in Eau Claire, Wisconsin: "We have an epidemic of obesity going on," she says. Obesity is defined as weighing 20 percent more than your ideal body weight, and things are especially heavy in Wisconsin. "We are trend leaders in obesity," says Dresel. "Although, I think we did drop to number two in the nation last year." To make matters worse, during winter in Wisconsin, most of us eat more and move less. Extra weight tends to stack up like snow in a supermarket parking lot, with one significant difference: Come springtime, the snow melts. Not so the accumulations of adiposity.

Of course, it isn't just the obese who fight the wintertime bulge. Ever since I got within a fork's length of 30, I've had an on-again, off-again relationship with an extra ten pounds. I don't obsess about it, but I do check the bathroom scale out of the corner of my eye now and again. I have been blessed with a metabolism that up to this point, at least, can be harassed into service, commandeered into burning away the winter's beltline buildup. But when it comes to people who eat too much, I have empathy — which, as any therapist worth their weight in diplomas will assure you is more important than sympathy. Because I love to eat. Oh, I eat my vegetables, and fiber is my friend. But nobody is a bigger fan of the empty calorie than yours truly. If it comes packaged in crinkly plastic, I'll eat it. If the sugar content hovers in the range of "pure cane octane," give me two. If artificial flavor is involved, so am I. And chocolate? Forget it. I've eaten enough chocolate in the past two years to double dip the Bloomer water tower like a big ol' marshmallow Easter egg.

And so, I have been approached by the editors of this magazine to address the problem in print. I'm sure they trust I will lend some sort of insight, tap some hidden source of knowledge, come up with nifty pun-intensive sidebars the likes of "Ten Sure-Fire Weighs (wink) to Drop Pounds Without Lifting a Finger."

I wish. I'd be on a national book tour so fast it would make your bathroom scale spin.

Oh, it's not as though you don't have options. Wisconsin may lead the way to the buffet, but the obsession with thinness is a national one, and it has spawned an industry eager to slim you down. Trouble is, no matter how honest they may be, somewhere along the line they all tend to have a ring of the snake oil salesman about them. According to one brochure, from a national weight loss organization, "...most diets allow just limited foods, and they don't teach you how to stay in control once you've lost weight." Of course, this begs the question: Do they offer a diet that allows *un*limited foods? Read on, and it sure sounds like it: "Our Fat & Fiber plan offers remarkable flexibility for those of you who need the freedom to eat just about anything, anywhere." Really. Well, make mine funnel cakes at the fair. More from the brochure: "...eat the foods you love while you follow our plan." Hmm. The foods I love — does your plan include chocolate-covered cherries and cheddarwurst?

When they're not making statements that stretch credulity, weight loss organizations often lapse into a fog of euphemisms. I've memorized a few, and intend to use them the next time I order breakfast at the local cafe: "And a lovely good morning to you, Cecille. Listen, as of this morning I am on a quest to make better food choices through problem-solving and goal-setting. I am seeking net physique enhancement. That being so, I am concerned with portion control and wish to avoid calorically dense foodstuffs, as well as significant fat sources. So whaddya got?" After a moment of silence, during which you could hear a fat-free corn curl drop, Cecille will probably shove a plateful of cheezy hash browns my way and say, "Here. Eat this. You'll feel better." And you know what? I will. And that's the problem. We love this stuff. It *does* make us feel better. That's what the dieters, dieticians, the diet centers, the weight counselors, the unsalted styrofoam chips, are up against. We know we should eat more fresh vegetables and less fat. But when's the last time you turned on the football game, kicked back the recliner, popped the top on a mineral water and proceeded to gorge yourself on celery sticks? Can you imagine tailgate parties at Lambeau Field featuring fiber? People arriving three hours before the game to fill galvanized stock tanks with icewater and mixed veggies? Stuffing down rice cakes and apple slices? I didn't think so.

Of course not everyone requires a national organization to lose weight. Americans are notorious for their do-it-yourself diets. All this self-starting can lead to trouble, however. "People tend to go on these crash diets," says Dresel. "They fast for a week. That's not going to work. You need to change your lifestyle." To make matters worse, dieters often gain more weight back than they originally lost — weight loss literature refers to this as the "yo-yo effect." And then there's this passage, a warning from another national weight reduction organization to amateur dieters everywhere: "Most dieters who achieve significant weight loss lose far too much lean body mass (muscle and organ tissue). This not only diminishes strength and agility but also affects appearance. With less muscle, pleasing curves flatten, chests sink; arms and legs look spindly." That does it. Pass the chicken-fried steak.

None of this is helped by the Wisconsin winter. Not only does the miserably cold weather make us want to eat, it makes us want to hibernate. Activity levels drop with the mercury.

So why fight it? Is thin all it's cracked up to be? You have to believe that the members of the National Association to Advance Fat Acceptance (NAAFA) were heartened by the recent Kate Moss controversy. You remember Kate Moss. She's the supermodel who looks like she just gave blood — all of it. Eyes like two vacant lots. A belly you could use to scoop bird seed. Kate caused a bit of controversy when a handful of social commentators commented that her popularity placed unrealistic pressure on American women to seek acceptance through thinness. Diane Dresel is all for thinness, but within reason. "We're not talking about making Twiggys [Twiggy was Kate Moss, circa the '60s] out of everybody. We're talking about a healthy lifestyle. Size acceptance is important. You need to accept people at any weight, like any height. Persons with weight problems are treated like second-class citizens. As a clinician, I'd like to see greater understanding of obesity. It's a chronic disease of lifestyle, the same as alcoholism. It has a high rate of relapse. If the alcoholic relapses and goes back to treatment, we say, 'good for you.' With weight, we tend to say the person has no self control or willpower. That's not the issue. We tell people you can like yourself but you don't have to like the weight." Perhaps some of this thinking is gaining a foothold: Lately, Kate Moss has been elbowed off the runway by wide-shouldered women with actual hips — not just hip *bones*. (It is interesting to note the part the weight loss industry plays in the Twiggy/Kate drama: Of 15 people pictured in the brochure of one national organization, 14 were women. The implicit message appears to be that it is less socially acceptable for a woman to be overweight than a man.)

So. You don't want the waif look, but you would like to fend off the ten pounds brought to you by Wisconsin delicacies and Wisconsin winter. What's the answer? Well, I've done all the research for you. I called experts, I read brochures, I looked in my refrigerator. Heck, I burned enough calories punching my way around the endless loop of the automated Weight Watchers® phone-mail system alone to earn myself a banana split (with a big white dose of that whipped cream in a can — a marvel of modern culinary engineering). But after all that work, I'm afraid what I have to say is less than thrilling. Whether you do it yourself or with the help of professionals, winter weight maintenance boils down to five words: *Eat less and move more.*

There you are. Plain and simple. Surely after all that talk about empty calories, you didn't think I'd sugarcoat it! 'Course, if I could get my hands on some chocolate. . . .

A DAY WITH DAVE

Dave Carlson is sincere. Simply that. He is sincere about the messages he shares via his regional television show, he is sincere in his words, and he is sincere in his deeds. Two days before I was to depart — solo — on a trip to Belize, he tracked me down with a phone call, quietly urging me to avoid a particularly troubled area. We had met only once before, on the day I was collecting material for this story. I went to the troubled area anyway — I had no choice — but I still remember the quiet concern in his voice. On the basis of a fleeting acquaintance, he took the time to warn me off a danger — to let me know I might come to harm. I ignored his instructions, but I got the message.

"LOOK OUT, DAVE!" Cameraman Tom Johnson is in the back seat of the maroon Jeep Cherokee, but out of habit, his eyes are on the road, which — should our present trajectory be maintained — we will shortly be leaving. A six-inch curb stands between us and an in-depth inspection of state highway department landscaping techniques.

Dave Carlson looks up from a bag of red licorice. He has been struggling to undo the twist tie. Now he tugs at the steering wheel and we juke to the left, temporarily back on course. "I saw it," says Carlson in a voice as tranquil as late summer backwater. We are still curling our way down the off-ramp, and he is already back at the twist tie.

When Dave Carlson was a Marine, he was given an aptitude test. One thing was certain, according to the clipped, uniformed man across the table: "You have no career in radio or television." *TV 13 Outdoors,* with Carlson at the helm, has now been on the air for fifteen years.

"I came here in 1981, on the day President Reagan was shot," says the softspoken host, who got his start as a reporter with the Eau Claire *Leader-Telegram*. "I was able to start an outdoor page there because I convinced some editors that people want to have this information and deserve to have this information. It puzzles me that you can have a newspaper like *USA Today* spend millions of dollars covering basically the jock sports — football, baseball, basketball, tennis, golf and so forth — yet they provide no routine, regular coverage of the outdoors. Just yesterday, on their own sports page, with a little "snapshot" type information graph, they reported that fishing was only behind walking, swimming and bicycling as the number one participatory sport in this country last year. Forty-five-and-a-half million people fish. Another 15 million hunt. I think that any newspaper that has an outdoors page finds that it's definitely of interest. And outdoors is not just hunting and fishing. It's the whole gamut of relating nature to the reader. Bird feeding, hiking, photography, biking — whatever — they all can be done within that arena of the outdoor page or the outdoor show."

Today Carlson is traveling to a section of the Mississippi near La Crosse for a story on river fishing. Specifically, he hopes to focus on techniques for landing river-dwelling smallmouth bass. The trip began like any other fishing trip: Three heavy-headed, sleep-deprived fishermen (including a man who responded only when addressed as "Porky") stuffing coolers, poles and tackle in the back of a pleasantly messy truck. There was the usual good-natured ribbing ("Cripes, what is all that stuff?!? It's not like we're going to Canada!!"), a special dose of which was reserved for the fourth member of the group, who appeared in the role of "the late guy." Of course, Tom Johnson may have been late, but since he was the only one amongst us who knew what all those camera buttons were for, he was in little danger of being left behind. Tipping back a slug of coffee from a well-worn camouflaged mug, Carlson backed out of the WEAU parking lot and we were on our way.

"This show is not about Dave Carlson being a professional fisher or hunter," says Carlson. "It's about people, places and things. Today we're after smallmouth in the Mississippi. Yesterday we profiled a woodcarver. It's the people's show. I'm just guarding it. At times it is a statement about my philosophy . . . but I am always conscious of the audience." And the audience is not who you might think it is. "Neilsen surveys of our program over the past 15 years — and I'm really happy about this — show that just slightly over half of our audience is women. That's important to me. And it's certainly important to advertisers. We don't target any specific audience, but those numbers tell me that we're putting out broad appeal programming.

"The most precious comments for me come from people who are casual, maybe occasional viewers of our shows and they say, 'I like it because it reminds me of things I remember from my youth,' or 'it reminds me of what my dad or mother or sister liked about the outdoors.' The other comment we hear is that it's refreshing. It's always different. And we struggle to make it that way."

"Whoa, lookit that!" Our heads swivel in unison, swinging right to sight two whitetails grazing just inside a pine copse at the edge of the interstate. Sunlit and hearty, they are a rusty red against the green of the morning. Carlson has seen thousands of these scenes in his time;

it reveals something about him that his head swung as eagerly as the rest of us. Of course, his head remains turned, and we begin to edge our way into the passing lane.

"I find it interesting to go out with the camera and absorb as much as I can and bring it back and sort through it and put the most meaningful stuff on the air," says Carlson. "Every day when I go in to edit the program, it's like creating a person. You start building in reverse. You build the skeleton, then you add the muscle. You put in the various organs, the heart and the brain and you breathe into it. And then you've created something that walks out amongst the public and they meet it and greet it and see it. And then it walks away."

The Jeep is winding its way through a small town. Pondside in a simple park, a gaggle of geese ruffle themselves against the morning. We meet a man in a clunky brown four-door, but after he passes, the streets stand empty. In the back seat, Porky is telling a Norwegian joke. Listening to Carlson, I miss the setup, and hear only the punch line: "Sven, Sven . . . where are you?" Tom Johnson leans against his door and laughs. It must have been a good one. Of course he also rolls his eyes — a not uncommon reaction to Norwegian jokes. Carlson has another piece of licorice.

Watching this man, his large, round features (including a mustache thick as a musky plug) sheltered under a comfortably faded Buck Knife cap, listening to his temperate voice with its trademark benedictory tone backed by the rattle of fishing poles, it is easy to see only a fisherman, to miss the fire that drives Dave Carlson. But while close calls on the highway hardly rate the slightest whitening of a knuckle, mention the environment, and Carlson leans forward, gripping the wheel tightly. In his voice, a bit of steel joins the velvet. "My personal philosophy is that everything emanates from the environment. If the environment is healthy, our people are healthy and our society is healthy. And right now I believe some things that are wrong with society are related to neglect of the environment. To me, overpopulation is the number one environmental problem." He slaps the wheel and sighs. "Oh, and then all of the other things we have done to the water, air and land. So I kind of keep those things in mind. . . . I try to peddle them right along with the other messages that we relate to the public — how to bait a hook, where to go pheasant hunting. I think we try to teach some environmental morality.

"I grew up in Gary, Indiana. The shores of Lake Michigan were so polluted that you could crush an alewife with every step. Now that lake is clear . . . so if that can be accomplished in an industrial setting, I guess there's hope. My biggest concern is that people not become apathetic . . . that they don't take the environment for granted. We cannot allow arrogant and greedy politicians to make decisions which have long-term implications for our resources. People become so disillusioned that they don't get involved in the Clean Water Act on a national level or endangered species, because they don't realize how it impacts locally. I can't do national in-depth documentaries, but I try to bring the essentials to the public's attention, and then try to incite them to think about it and act."

In LaCrosse, we are on another exit ramp. Carlson is sharing a story with Porky, who is seated directly behind him. He addresses Porky

in the rearview mirror. We drift across the white centerline. "Dave . . . ,"
says Johnson.

As an avowed environmentalist, Carlson acknowledges that he
faces a dilemma in the Lucky 13 fishing and hunting contests associ-
ated with his show. "First of all, I'm a very strong advocate of catch
and release . . . that does not mean that I don't think people shouldn't
be able to keep and kill fish. The station started that contest 35 years
ago, and quite frankly I've tried pretty hard and sometimes been taken
to task for trying to minimize the contest as part of the show. The same
thing for the big buck contest in the fall. But on the other hand, I look
at the mounds of entries to the fishing contest, and I have I try to look
at this way . . . chances are many of those fish would have been kept
anyhow. And I'm also enough of a realist to know that not all of the
fish that are big that are kept are entered in our contest." He chuckles
ruefully. "I guess I sometimes go to bed and I see fish swimming by,
pointing a finger at me. . . . "

When we arrive at the river, we are split between two power boats.
The guide keeps the 150 horse motor throttled to a good-natured
chuckle as we pass through a "no-wake" passage lined with boathouses
that date back to the 1930s. Back to the prow, Carlson engages the guide
in a discussion that ranges from fish kills to river sedimentation to
zebra mussels. As we pass under an old "twist" bridge (with two hours
warning, the entire bridge can be twisted on its piling to allow a tall
boat to pass) reeking of creosote, the no-wake zone ends. The guide
punches the throttle and soon we are capless, the wind snapping our
ears. A mile down the river, the guide kills the engine and we drift

across a wing dam. The boat is still in motion and Carlson is stripping line from his fly rod. In no time at all, he has snagged a tree. I know it is small of me, and mean, but this makes me feel great.

Of course things don't always go smoothly. In addition to snagging trees, Carlson has snagged himself. Right in the ear, out in the middle of nowhere, in Montana. Carlson chuckles. "I hollered at my fishing partner, told him, 'Doc, you have to do some surgery.'

"We've had some close calls. A near sinking on Lake Superior, once. Could have been a dangerous situation — it wasn't. I've been bowled over by bear, I've been peed on by a timber wolf pup. Of course I've been hooked, I've been scratched, I've been cut, I've been bumped, dropped — and I've bumped and dropped and bowled over other people. I've spilled things, I've started little fires, I've broken I don't know how many rods and lost more baits than I care to talk about."

When asked to describe the highlight of his television career, Carlson makes an interesting choice. "Like a lot of the public, I struggled with the whole Chippewa spearfishing issue[1], and I tried to remain extremely neutral on the air, as well as at any public appearances I made where I was asked about it. Those years were awfully tough on the state and the people of the state saw some of the most . . . [here Carlson took a long pause] . . . *terrible* behavior by people that I've ever seen without things getting violent. I'm glad it's over. . . .

---

[1]During the 19th century, the U.S. Government and the Ojibwe Nation, commonly known as the Chippewa, negotiated several treaties, which (among other things) gave the U.S. vast tracts of land in Wisconsin and gave the Ojibwe rights to various natural resources, including the right to harvest fish by spear from many Wisconsin lakes. In the 1980s, this treaty right became a divisive issue between Indians and whites in northern Wisconsin, particularly between sport fishermen and the Lac Courte Oreilles band of the Ojibwe.

"So that was kind of a highlight, covering that and maintaining neutrality, which is what you're paid to do and expected to do. Getting the story out even though you know it was very offensive to some people. Very offensive, at times, to both sides. But we did our best to get it out."

The smallmouth are parsing out their visits to our boats in lean form. Johnson, with little to film, smokes a cigarette while Carlson describes a recent unsuccessful fishing trip. "...second time in 56 trips to Canada I didn't catch a walleye," he says. Then he reveals his writer's flair for words, describing weather which left the water "oily flat." It is a wonderfully apt description. I file it away. In good time I will steal it for my own.

Porky is telling another joke. "Hear the one about the happy fisherman? He found out his wife had worms!" Porky is what you would call a "character."

"Time for more licorice," says Carlson, placing his fly rod on the deck. I have noticed Carlson eating the licorice in a methodical way, as if it is the process, not the act, of eating he is after. When he reveals late in the day that he recently gave up a longtime pipe smoking habit, I understand.

"I'm a realist about my job," says Carlson. "My wife is a nurse. She has been a nurse for 26 years. She deals with life and death situations every week. How does my job stack up to that?!? It means nothing, comparatively. What it does have is the power to inform, possibly to educate, and to entertain people. I realize there is immense power there. I try not to abuse it, and hopefully for a few minutes on Sunday night, make life a little better for people."

In the end, we caught enough fish and learned enough about the river to turn the trip into a useful segment for the coming weekend's show. It was out of the water and back on the road. "I've traveled seven-and-a-half million miles on this job," says Carlson, speaking with both hands, which only occasionally graze the steering wheel. "Fourteen states, four Canadian provinces, Belize...." Tom Johnson points out that Carlson has just driven past the on-ramp. Pulling over, Carlson backs the Cherokee along the shoulder to reconnoiter the missed exit. Then, red licorice clamped in his teeth, he veers down the ramp, taking the curve in segments, headed for an even 8 million.

PEOPLE TO AVOID
ON THE BACKPACK CIRCUIT

*I've seen a bunch of territory with my backpack right behind me.
Fifteen or sixteen countries, something like that. Last winter, I moseyed
around Central America. Actually, I went to Belize for two weeks, but it
sounds so much more intriguing to say Central America. Conjures up
visions of revolution, drug smuggling, and Harrison Ford. Anyway, I had
my backpack, and I ran into some other folks with backpacks, and soon I
began to notice things. Those things are listed below.*

So you've decided to stuff your life in a reinforced nylon box and
hoof it for hostel world — travel by foot and thumb, amble the
backroads with nary a care, nary a plan, nary a feeling in your arms,
the straps are digging in that hard. But be forewarned: tribulation (and
a permanent subscapular cramp the size of a volleyball) awaits the
backpacker! Never mind the wild-eyed street hustlers, the crack-addled
pickpockets or the Kalashnikov-toting teenage border guards. They
may chase you down the street, finger your lint, or confiscate your
passport and string you up by the thumbs, but they'll rarely stand on
your face to reach the top bunk, prattle on until 3 a.m. about the meaning of life and a psychic aunt in Des Moines, or throw up on your
sleeping bag — unlike your fellow travelers, classified and listed as
follows:

❖ The long-skirted Earth Mother. A vastly patient spirit. Speaks in
the earnest monotones of a third-rate folk singer reciting a poem written by a third-grader about a dead dog. Likely to trigger repressed

memories of support groups and bad incense. Certain to be outfitted with a hand-made Guatemalen tote bag. Finds wonder in all things. Badgers you to accept a copy of a cancer-curing plaintain poultice recipe channeled to her in a daydream by an eighth-century Mayan faith healer. Look lady, I'll sort my cans, I'll cut back on the beef, and I'll even hang a dream catcher from the rear-view mirror, but in the meantime aren't you late for a harmonic convergence somewhere?

❖ The "where-the-hell's McDonald's" guy. Say no more. More than likely, there's a backwards baseball cap involved.

❖ Rich kids with gear. A particularly revolting strain of happy camper. Usually reeking with an air of self-sacrifice, positively edematous with pride over their willingness to mingle with quaint third-world beggar types. Generally packing things like miniature triple-locking machine-knurled aquamarine carabiner keychains, portable campfire espresso maker with brass steam pipe and oscillating rescue strobe, and fully digital titanium insect repellent dispensers. "Look Mummy — it's got 100% DEET!"

❖ The Boobs of Berlitz. These are people determined to inflict their hack native tongue despite the native's desire to communicate in English, in which the native has been fluent since the age of three. The Boobs of Berlitz are easily recognized. They generally walk around with their finger stuck up their phrase book.

❖ Multi-lingual, historically- and geographically-informed Europeans. These people make you feel ignorant and inferior. As well they should.

Now then. Excoriating these folks without affording them the opportunity to defend themselves is hardly sporting. But it is certainly good fun. To prevent my completely alienating anyone who ever hoisted a pack, however, I reckon it prudent that I answer the question, "OK Mr. Crabby Pants, where do you fit on the list?" And then I must admit that at any given time, I can be placed in nearly all of the above categories. I mean, I'm no earth mother, but on a recent backpacking trip to Belize, I did pack a tube of camper's biodegradable soap. Great stuff. Smells like coconuts. Gives you that fresh, clean feeling, as if you've been scrubbed with . . . coconuts. As far as the McDonald's guy, well, I was doing just great, eating nothing but jungle rat and unidentified tubers, until that lonely afternoon in Orange Walk Town when I spotted a woman selling Snickers bars. . . . And I'm certainly no rich kid, but I do have gadget disease. Got me a portable water purifier before I left. Aw, it's great. Top o' the line. Fits right in the backpack. Tubes, plungers, little hoses, charcoal filters, the works. This thing would separate Rush Limbaugh from a box of chocolates. Of course it never came out of the box. They may be a third-world country, but they got bottled water. I don't carry phrase books, so I'm not really a Berlitz boob, but I did once spend five minutes dancing around a small post office in rural Germany, holding a postcard in my teeth, flapping my arms and saying "luft!" over and over. Eventually the postmistress looked at me and said, "Air Mail?"

Which brings me back to those self-satisfied, smug Europeans. That's the one group in which I can't claim membership. But I expect the look of smug will soon be replaced by the look of mouth breather. On what do I construct my thesis? Why, the fact that the most popular television show in Europe is . . . *Baywatch*. For the moment, they're multilingual. But when we get done implanting Pamela Anderson in their national semi-consciousness, I expect their love of language, history and culture will rapidly devolve into monosyllabic ruminations on re-runs. And then, finally, there will exist among the tromping ranks of backpacking a subgroup which we can approach without trepidation and compare subscapular cramps.

WORKIN' ON THE ROAD GANG

Middle of North Dakota, 2 a.m., eastbound on 94, a few years back. The northern lights were alive, iridescing across the sky like oil across water. Punching the buttons, trying to catch some "skip," I heard an old country song. Halfway through, the music broke up and faded to static. I continued down the dial, and heard the song again. This time, I locked the button and the signal remained strong. As the song ended, an air horn sounded, and a man sang out, "Hey! You're on the Road Gang!"

Nashville. Just past midnight. The Country Music Hall of Fame is closed. Music Row is empty. The tourists who dawdle up and down Demonbreun Street during the day are tucked in their motels. But if you wait a moment, let your ears sort the sounds of night, you can hear the big rigs pulling I-40. A block from the Hall of Fame, inside the studios of WLAC, Dave Nemo looks at the red second hand sweeping across the large wall clock above his head and punches the microphone button. "Hope you'll stay with us while we go truckin' into Tuesday." He inserts what looks like a miniature 8-track tape into a machine. The tape is actually called a "cart," and it contains a 30-second commercial. While the spot plays, Nemo selects the next cart from a rack of several hundred. As the final commercial concludes, Nemo pops in one last cart, slides the volume control up, and the jingle I first heard on that North Dakota highway fills the studio: "Hey! You're on the Road Gang!"

Dave Nemo works in a space not much bigger than a semi cab. In place of a steering wheel, his fingers skip around a console studded with faders and blinking lights. He remains standing throughout the entire show, often in a pair of tennies, wearing a pair of $13.95 Radio Shack headphones he bought for his wife in the '70s. While the stereotypical radio personality is either loud, cocky, controversial, or possessed of a voice that can loosen lugnuts at fifty paces, Nemo is none of these things. He describes his voice as "light," and his tone is strictly conversational. He never sounds as if he's hyping his show or his listeners; rather, he chats as if he were riding shotgun in each rig that tunes him in, making conversation to pass the miles, to ward off sleep. His hair is light and sandy, and is the type often described as "thinning." A trim gray beard circles his chin. He has the look of a guy you'd see buying a garden hose in Wal-Mart on a Saturday.

Early in each show, Nemo generally discovers an item of sufficient interest to elicit a few phone calls. Occasionally a topic will take on a life of its own, and carry over from show to show. Tonight a bit of news catches Nemo's eye. It seems the Rock and Roll Hall of Fame is outfitted with musical ATM machines. Over the air, Nemo wonders aloud what music would be appropriate for a cash machine. Soon the calls are stacking up.

Steve, in Waverly, Iowa: "How 'bout 'Busted?'"

John in Mt. Shasta: "I'd pick 'Money Makes the World Go 'Round,' from *Cabaret*."

Jeff, from an oil platform in the Gulf of Mexico: "'Lord Have Mercy on the Workin' Man.'"

"Spinnerbait" ("they call me that 'cause I'd rather be fishin'") calls

from Huntsville, on his way to Houston: "Yeah, I say, 'If You've Got . . .'"
Nemo interrupts him. "Wait a minute, man, don't even tell me. I'll have
you come on the air when we get out of the commercial break." When
the commercial is over, Nemo patches the trucker's call into the broad-
cast, and he submits what eventually becomes the evening's most popular ATM song, "If You've Got the Money, I've Got the Time." He and
Nemo sing a few bars, and then Nemo taps a computer keyboard and
begins reading the Interscan weather reports.

While the weather and road reports can provide truckers with critical information, they're also a form of geographical poetry. It's com-
forting, when the white lines are flicking by in the night, to listen as
Nemo recites: "Hagerstown to Harrisburg, light fog ... Gary to Decatur,
clear ... Moses Lake and Mullen reporting showers ... Albert Lea to
Lemoyna, scattered slippery spots ... Breezewood to Baltimore, clear
and dry..." America is shrouded in darkness, but Nemo's recitation
conjures up an image of a country united by specific places and the
roads that connect them.

George "Tex" Samler, an owner/operator leased to Transport
America, has been on those roads for 31 years. Ask what kind of music
he likes, and he replies in one emphatic word: "Rock!" And yet, he's
been listening to Dave Nemo's country show since Nemo came on the
air in 1972. Why? "Dave knows what it's like out there, what we're
doing, and the problems that we all face every day." It is this acceptance by truckers that has allowed Nemo — never a trucker himself —
to stay on the air all these years, and he knows it. "I've been very fortunate," says Nemo, but it's no secret that respect for his audience plays
a large part in that acceptance. And that respect is genuine. You can
hear it tonight during the road report as Nemo describes an overturned

tanker on I-95, leaking 8,000 gallons of fuel. If this were a rush-hour traffic report, the tanker would be one more commuter inconvenience, one more slowdown on the road home. When Nemo shares the news with the Road Gang, the impact is much different. His audience doesn't think of the traffic, they think of the trucker. As he backs away from the mike, it's easy to imagine truckers all across the nation taking a little firmer grip on the wheel.

For Nemo, the road to the Road Gang began in Louisiana. "I worked my way through school out on the riverfront in New Orleans, making tow and playing in a country music band. There were 9,000 rock bands and two country bands — if you played country, you had a lot of work! When I was a senior in college, I got a part-time job at WWL in New Orleans. This is 1969, and my lottery number was 17, so I enlisted in the Army. I wound up at Yong Song base in Seoul, Korea on the air with a program called "Nemo's Nightbeat." When I came back to New Orleans and WWL in 1972, the Road Gang had started up, and I joined the show because of my country music background." And how long does Nemo intend to lead the Road Gang? He laughs. "Until they shoot me."

At 4:20 a.m., the ATM song suggestions are still coming, and Nemo is still answering the phone like he's at a clubhouse, not at work: "Hi, Road Gang, Dave here!" Before he hangs up, he always asks, "Where are ya?" Back on the air, he leans into the mike and recites the call letters and frequencies of the Road Gang stations. And then, from his tiny co-driver's console just off I-40, Dave Nemo speaks to his driving partners all across the American nightscape:

"Punch those numbers in . . . we don't want to get separated in the dark."

SAVING THE KIDNEYS

Maybe this piece shouldn't be in here. It's been rejected a number of times. Each time, the criticism it received was virtually identical. Everyone seems to approve of the description of the main character and his work, but they want to know more about the relationship between the main character and his daughter.

I think they're right. That dimension of the story that is undeniably thin. But y'know what? This man consented to have me tag along while he worked. He shared what he wanted to share. And there is no compelling reason for me to push into his life any further. So...I include this as it is. Not out of spite, but because Paul Nickles works hard at an unusual job, and I thought you might like to hear about it. Besides, I nearly froze my nose.

The first thing you notice is the momentum. The slaughter trailer resembles a rolling derrick, all steel and cable, and as you hurtle through the swampland in the cab of the battered brown pickup to which it is hitched, the trailer feels as if it is pushing more than being pulled, its impatient weight nudging at your back even as you try to outrun it. Paul Nickles pushes the truck hard. The engine maintains a steady roar, the heavy tires growl and whine, changing key to the tune of the road. He brakes for corners only when it seems the entire rumbling conglomeration must surely launch itself deep into the bracken. The brakes grate, the truck shudders, the turn is rounded and the accelerator flattened once again; the tattered brown truck flaps its wooden side racks, gathers its resources and surges out of the curve. As soon as the speed levels off, the slaughter trailer resumes its nudging.

Nickles looks over. "Vacation day today!" He grins, wide open.

His pale blue eyes are direct, unwavering even when they sparkle, which is often. "I'm takin' off to go to the Cities this afternoon." Later I will learn that the afternoon trip to Minneapolis is for a doctor's appointment. Nickles' six-year-old daughter is in chronic renal failure; her one kidney, taken from Paul's older brother, who is also a butcher, is working, but there is trouble ahead.

"Vacation day, Sunday, it don't matter. I've been on Christmas. I butchered one one hour after my daughter was born," Nickles chuckles, his grin undimmed. "Boss called me at the hospital. Wife wasn't too happy, but I told her, 'Hey, most guys go to the bar!'" He cocks both eyebrows, and the grin becomes knowing.

Nickles was 14 when he first began work at the meat market. "I started as a cleanup boy, and worked my way up the ladder. By the time I was 16 I was on the kill floor." He still works full-time at the shop; the traveling butcher role is a private enterprise. "The guy who started the mobile slaughter unit moved to Texas, so I took over," Nickles says, leaning into a curve, glancing briefly at the road ahead. Now he is on call 24 hours a day, ready to respond to farmers hoping to salvage a down or injured animal. Not all of his customers approach him in an emergency; a certain number of his visits are scheduled. "Some folks feel better about having their animal killed where it lived," says Nickles. There is no trace of irony in his voice.

Nickles' part-time assistant, George, sits between Nickles and me. Mostly he is silent. When he does speak, it is mostly in the form of colorful interjection. "Biggest animal we ever did?" says Nickles, "eleven-seventy five, dressed out. Whitefaced steer."

George stirs. "And that's without the heart, tongue and liver."

We are at the crossroads of a small northern town, surrounded by pines. A butcher from a neighboring town is to meet us here, lead us to a farm where two hogs wait. Paul pulls into the parking lot of a shuttered drive-in diner. It is hard to imagine rolled-down windows and corn dogs this morning; as the engine dies, the heat in the cab seeps away almost audibly. It is 7:30 a.m., and the sun has been up a while, but the temperature is locked at an intractable 15 degrees below zero.

"A warm winter, you'll see more emergency calls," says Nickles. He is leaning forward, tapping the wheel, looking west down the highway, impatient for the butcher. "It gets warm, they turn the cows out, then it freezes up and they slip and fall. Get a lot of broken legs, split pelvics. There he is." He twists the ignition. The butcher waves, and we pull in behind him.

The farm is far from town, a small set of isolated buildings hunkered against the cold. As we round the turn at the end of a long drive, a cat goes stock-still in mid-step, stares for a split second, then reverses itself, flashing out of sight behind a grain bin. Paul sizes up the layout, choosing an approach that will allow him access to the barn, but there is more to it. "Gotta think about how you're going to get back out," he says. "It'd be nice if all you had to do was shoot it and stick it, but y'never know. Might have to drag it around three corners."

George is grinning. "We had to hook one on the barn cleaner chain once."

"There, that'll work," says Nickles. "No power lines." The truck stops, the engine is switched off, and he is already gone, rifle tucked under his arm. In a clean pen, a pig grunts inquisitively as we enter the barn. The pig is on its feet when Nickles opens the gate, and the 'whap!' of the shot is immediate. There is no talk, no prelude. The pig drops without a sound and Nickles is upon it, lancing the jugular with a short, swift stab. The blood rolls out, and Nickles moves to the next pen, where the process is repeated.

George has followed with two oversized bale hooks. He gives one to Nickles and the two men snag a pig each, inserting the hook through the underside of the jaw, in the same way a fisherman baits a hook with a minnow. The pigs are slid from the pen, down the manger, and into the yard. Nickles positions the trailer boom and grabs a knife. As he bends to the upended pig and begins to remove its forefeet, he addresses the butcher. "Went bowlin' for the fire department last night." He circles each leg with the knife, then grasps the hoof. With a twist of his wrist, he snaps the foot free, tossing it aside. "Bowled a 256 the first game, ended up with a 591." He hasn't looked up. He slits the pig's skin down the midline from chin to groin, then runs the knife inward from each leg, angling in to the midline cut. He has stopped speaking now, pausing only to slap his flat, curved knife across the sharpener. In the wind, the metallic scraping sounds as if it is coming from a culvert.

I have ducked behind the corner of the garage, looking for relief from the gusts which sweep up through the barnyard from a bowl-like depression where the pasture unrolls to the distant wood. The morning weatherman warned of dangerous windchills in the -30 degree range. It is all that and more. I have three pens, which I rotate through my front pants pocket, deep beneath my coveralls. A fresh pen lasts for six medium-sized words. Nickles continues to dissect the pig. He is barehanded.

George picks up the four feet, throws them in a barrel at the front of the trailer. Pulling a knife from a bucket, he cuts out the pig's tongue. He hefts it, then it joins the feet.

Nickles straightens. He inserts his bloody hands in a pair of stained florescent orange gloves before picking up a large, electric meat saw. "Don't wanna touch metal," he says, grinning again. With a quick dip of the saw, he bisects the sternum. "Take'er up, George!"

The winch chatters and complains, but the hog rises, hoisted by its hocks. When it is chest high, Nickles reaches into the abdomen and pulls out reams of pale white intestines. "This is the best part of the job," he grins. "Hands're warm!" On the ground, the blood freezes so quickly little of it seeps into the snow. It is a dusky, purplish red; in the wind, our stiff faces assume the same hue.

When the pig is cleanly eviscerated, Paul again dons his gloves and hoists the saw. It has frozen, and he works it back and forth until it breaks free. Beginning at the tail, he halves the pig, drawing the saw downward, stopping just short of the nose. Now Paul, George and the butcher wrestle the V'd pig into a large plastic bag which balloons and crackles in the wind. As they heave the pig toward the butcher's truck, the men are thrown off balance. The hooks have frozen in the hocks. The boom is lowered, and with much grunting, the hooks are twisted free. The pig disappears into the truck bed.

The second pig goes even more quickly. George helps by kneeing the hide away from the suspended body. I notice the kidneys remain in each pig. "I pop'em and leave'em in the carcass," says Paul. "Gotta leave'em for the state inspector." The kidneys are used to gauge the general health of the animal; scarring or other abnormalities indicate an underlying problem, and the meat may be condemned. In some cases, the twin organs are so visibly damaged that Nickles condemns the animal on the spot. Farmers losing a hog this way have been known to curse him roundly; of course they do not realize how well Nickles understands the price of bad kidneys.

Soon we are back on the road. Our second appointment, a single hog, is 30 miles away. I express surprise at the speed of the butchering process compared to time spent on the road. "Hogs, we've done five an hour," says Nickles. I ask him about the process of killing an animal. "I'd rather shoot a pig with'em lookin' at me," he says. Again, there is no irony in his voice. "Sometimes if you shoot'em behind the ear, the bullet goes all the way through and ricochets around the barn." Indeed, at our next appointment, the bullet left the pig's skull and dented the gate.

Whereas the first farm we visited was neat and spare, the second was cluttered and largely in disrepair. The wind hurled itself unchecked through gaping holes in the haymow. In the yard it whipped and twisted through a maze of pallet stacks, discarded truck parts and outdated speedboats. We found the pig easily, but the farmer refused to have it shot in the barn. "He doesn't want blood in there," said Paul. "It can get the other pigs to attack each other." Three feet outside the barn door, the pig blinks and snuffles in the light, and turns toward Nickles. Whap.

Nickles has killed thousands of animals. He has no specific number, just "thousands." Yet, skinning another steaming pig, he hardly personifies death, clad as he is in a faded orange snow suit, one leg of which is held together by copious twists of silver duct tape. Contrary to the popular perception of the burly butcher, Nickles is a slight man. His hands are scarred and thickened enough to reflect his profession, but his gold wedding band fits loosely over a small ring finger. Even a dark ski mask fails to lend an air of the sinister. Except when he is in the teeth of the wind, the mask is pushed up from his face, piled atop his head in loose rolls, a lackadaisical turban.

On the way home, the turban is riding high, and Nickles is in a storytelling mood. "Wanna hear a myth?" He grins for the fortieth time that day. "I knew an old farmer could predict the winter by the spleen of a hog. You fold the spleen in half. That's halfway through winter. Then you measure the width and the thickness from there. This winter was supposed to be warm in the middle, then get cold with a lot of precipitation." It is exactly the kind of winter we have had.

"Have I ever shot the wrong animal? Yes. Farmer said, 'That's the one...I think.' By the time he said 'I think' it was too late." His grin grows wider, and he shoots a sidelong glance. "Don't say, 'I think'!"

"Sometimes this is like a rodeo. I been chased. Two weeks ago, one of Scooter Shystacker's longhorns, she was temper-mental — that's why they had her done — come after me. Run her horns along that gate like a kid with a stick. She came after me and I jumped up in the truck and shot her."

"Sheep now, in the slaughterhouse, we use electrocution," he continues. George perks up.

"'Member that time I shocked one, and four of'em dropped?"

"I've done C-sections," says Paul. "In a cow, you've got two minutes. I like to get'em out in about 45 seconds. You've got to tie the umbilical cord off and cut it, and then slit the cow's throat. It's kind of a good thing to bring one in the world after all the ones I've taken out."

As we near town, talk turns to Nickles' daughter. "She's six years old and weighs 30 pounds," he says. "Her kidneys were all full of scar tissue." He gives a detailed report of the surgeries she has undergone, the medications she must take daily to maintain her fragile state. "She's died on us twice," he says. "One time at home. I gave her CPR. It's a day-to-day thing."

It's still only 11:00 a.m. when we turn off Main Street and back the trailer behind the shop. Nickles disappears inside as I gather my things. As I step to the door to thank him, it swings open with a rush, and he strides into the cold sunlight. "Got another one!" he says. "Over by New Richmond!"

It is a fair distance to New Richmond. I ask if there will be time to do this and still make the two-hour drive to the hospital in Minneapolis. He answers over his shoulder, on the move.

"I think I can make it!"

Of course, he is grinning.

THE FAT MAN DELIVERS CHRISTMAS

December, 1994. Two weeks before Christmas. The Fat Man and I roll into Hendersonville, Tennessee. We're hauling precious cargo, and the townsfolk line up along Highway 31 to wave us in. They get right up close, but I believe I have the best view, right there in the plate-sized rear-view mirror of that Silver Eagle: 53 tour buses, ponderous and sleek (most belonging to country music artists, but a few the property of drivers on the NASCAR circuit), curving out of sight behind us, snaking through the darkness like a giant string of holiday lights towed down the slow lane by the very hand of God. Garth's bus is back there, and Wynonna's. Reba sent one, and so did Brooks & Dunn. The marquees at the brow of each vehicle read like the weekly Top 40. But this parade isn't about big names. This parade is about kids, and Christmas. And it's about people like the Fat Man.

The bus driver they call the Fat Man was born Gene Reed. Been driving a bus for 31 years. He's hauled Ferlin Huskey, Nat Stuckey, George Jones, Mel Tillis, the Forrester Sisters, Joe Stampley, Brother Phelps, Ricky Van Shelton, Van Halen, Kiss, 2 Live Crew, MC Hammer, Boyz II Men. Voice like a Dixie backroad: all gravel and drawl. A raconteur's love of holding the stage. Quick on the trigger with an infinite range of ripostes, nearly all of them unprintably earthy. And one of the founders of "Christmas Is for Kids," the event that drew me to Hendersonville. "Christmas Is for Kids" began in 1981 when Reed and a group of nine buses arranged to transport 25 disadvantaged children to a special Christmas dinner and shopping trip. The volunteer efforts of the drivers, artists, and chaperones, combined with the cooperation of regional school officials eventually transformed the first humble outing into a major event. The buses rolling through Hendersonville tonight carry 358 children. "We pick up our kids and meet at the First Baptist Church," says the Fat Man. "The church puts on a meal and entertainment. Santa Claus is there. Then we come on up here with these buses in a convoy. And man, they give us the street."

Outside my window, a parked pickup truck beeps and flashes its lights. Our three young passengers are in the rear of the bus — site of the artist's master bedroom — watching cartoons, so I wave from the co-pilot seat in their place. A small part of me hopes I'll be taken for a star.

Before we set off in convoy, the children were given an after-dinner tour of Trinity City. Formerly known as Twitty City, in honor of Conway Twitty, whose home was on the grounds, the expansive complex was soaked in white Christmas lights; every tree was incandescent, every structure was outlined in twinkles. I kept hearing the words, "Look! Look!" The children wound their way around flickering garden paths, across miniature walk bridges spanning a manicured stream, through sheltered courtyards. Fairy tale scenes were arranged in diorama at each bend in the path. Many of the children chattered noisily. Some darted out of line. A pair of children in snow jackets left the tour to fool around in a garbage can. A tiny child, hand engulfed by a driver's beefy palm, stood transfixed in the face of it all, head tipped back, mouth parted, eyes wide. I looked at that child, and my throat hurt.

We left through tall gates and walked to the buses.

A lengthy wait ensued while the convoy was organized and the police escort arranged itself. Our kids wrestled in the aisle, and Reed spotted them in the mirror. "Awright, you kids, cut it out 'fore I snatch y'nekkid n'blister yer butt!" The giggling never let up as they ran off to the television in the back of the bus, to watch *The Simpsons*. Impatient, Reed keyed his CB mike and sang, "Sha na na na, Sha na na na, move'em on out." A sardonic drawl came back at him: "What'd you do with the money I sent you for singin' lessons?" Reed cut him off. "I took your wife out, and I shoulda took the singin' lessons!" He turned to me. "I guess he'll ask me *that* again." Throughout the evening, the CB babble of boisterous good ol' boy bluster never stopped. We finally got the OK to head out. Reed celebrated the move with a heartfelt ditty: "Rollin', rollin', rollin', although my ass is swollen..." The kids were still in the back.

Out on the road, the CB traffic continued.

"I'm on the right side of ya, hauler!"

"Don't put no Prevost bus in there!"

"Let's slow'em down, get'em t'gether, tighten up!"

"Them Prevost, they'll run ya crazy!"

"Aw, yer a walkin' crime against nature!"

"Slow'em down up there, slow'em down!"

"OK, awright."

We wound around a long bend and Reed pointed out the door to the mirror. "That's a mess o' buses, buddy."

The convoy reaches the Kmart on the east end of town. The buses arrange themselves diagonally, in rows. The children are met by volunteer chaperones and taken to the store. The previous evening, in the same parking lot, the public was allowed to poke around the buses, examine the airbrushed murals, plush carpets, gleaming make-up mirrors. The accumulated funds finance a shopping spree for each child. The Fat Man shakes his head. "You'd think you'd hand a child $50, $75, the first place they'd head would be the toy department. But most of'em won't buy no toys — they'll buy'em somethin' to wear...a pair of shoes...it's just somethin' amazing to watch, man. It kinda restores your faith."

It's not all joyous. Some of the older kids know what's going on. Inside the store, their gaze slides to the tiles if they catch you looking. They hunch their shoulders a bit, move over an aisle. A photographer has accompanied me on the trip. He has taken pictures of the buses, the convoy. Inside the Kmart, he can't bring himself to uncap his lens. But back on the bus, the little girl who has been riding with us rushes aboard to show her purchases, and her eyes are clear and bright as she displays a necklace for her teacher, a trinket for her brother. She allows as how she can't wait to give them away, and then bounces back to watch cartoons again. Her bag remains on the table. In addition to a few toys, it contains socks, a shirt, a pair of mittens. The Fat Man was halfway through a decidedly ribald anecdote when the little girl returned. He draws a slow breath. "You really wanna see happiness in sadness, pain and sufferin' turned to smiles. . . . " He trails off, the sentence, like the anecdote, left unfinished.

The Fat Man drops me off back at the First Baptist parking lot. In the rear of the bus, the children are dancing around the bed. They holler a Merry Christmas at the photographer and me, then go back to dancing. The photographer and I will drive all night. We have to be in northern Wisconsin by morning. "Keep'er outta the buckwheat," hollers The

Fat Man. He waves, and the pneumatic door closes with a hiss. The air brakes release, and the diesel swells. The bus swings in a wide circle and glides away.

Somewhere in the middle of the night, I suppose about Indiana, I tell the photographer about the child with the wide eyes. How I was suddenly at the edge of tears over the simple wonder of the image. I tell him how I can't get around the troubling thought that this night of fantasy might only highlight troubles at home. I tell him how I can't understand why all this goodness leaves me unsettled. The Fat Man sees happiness in sadness . . . somehow I've gotten it backward.

They came to Hendersonville again this year. Fifty-one buses. Three-hundred-and-two children. And the Fat Man was there. He'd driven 165,000 miles since his last Christmas Is for Kids. Enough mileage to circle the earth six times and most of a seventh; endless miles spent fighting inclement weather, artless motorists, clutch-shredding grades . . . the clock. But when he pulled that land yacht into line and rolled it sweet and easy up Highway 31, it was smooth sailing.

Man, they gave'em the street.

ABOUT THE AUTHOR

Michael Perry was raised on a small farm in northwestern Wisconsin. He has written for publications ranging from Newsweek to the New York Times Magazine to The Christian Science Monitor to Cowboy Magazine, and his essays and humor are heard on both Wisconsin and Minnesota public radio. When he's not contributing articles to magazines, Perry contributes humor to the local fire department by being the first volunteer fireman in village history to miss the monthly meeting because of a poetry reading.

To order additional copies of this book,
send $9.95 per book, plus $2.50 shipping and handling, to
Whistlers & Jugglers Press
P.O. Box 1346
Eau Claire, WI 54702-1346

ALSO AVAILABLE by Michael Perry

NEVER STAND BEHIND A SNEEZING COW

a live-audience recording of Perry filing humorous reports
from the fictional town of Foggy Crossing on the topics of
Fightin' Frogs football
parade floats gone bad
slide shows as sleep aids
coon dogs and the people who own them
critical elements of manure-spreader maintenance
fire-department raffles
things you should never say on an ambulance
Mavis Turner's homemade *Love Guide*
and of course, this business about the cow

Send $9.95 per cassette, plus $2.50 shipping and handling, to
Whistlers & Jugglers Press
P.O. Box 1346
Eau Claire, WI 54702-1346